QUIRX:

With no brothers or sisters, ~~~~ read hungrily as a child, wrote stories rather ~~~~ her father's old typewriter (which made for lots of mistakes) and was sole proprietor of the weekly magazine, *Lesley's Gazette*, popular with her teachers at primary school! After growing up and moving to the west country, Lesley had many different jobs. She worked in two market gardens, a pottery and a residential home for the elderly – as well as picking daffodils in the beautiful Tamar Valley, the inspiration for her first published novel, *The Flower King*, shortlisted for both the Guardian Children's Fiction Award and the Whitbread Children's Novel Award.

Since then her second book, *MapHead*, has won the 1995 Guardian Children's Fiction Award and has been shortlisted for the Writers' Guild Children's Book Award, the Carnegie Medal, the Young Telegraph Award and the W. H. Smith Mind Boggling Books Award. She has also written *Weather Eye*, which won the Smarties Book Prize (9–11 category), *The Pits* and *MapHead 2*.

Having started out writing with short stories, Lesley quickly rediscovered how much fun they were – and how badly these quirky stories wanted to jump out of their box! Gaining inspiration from everyday life has always been a major interest. From supermarkets to Avon ladies, dentists to school bus drivers, there's nothing stranger than truth, as they say – or at least, an off-the-wall view of it! The first volume of *Quirx – Welcome to Inner Space*, is available from Hodder Children's Books.

Lesley Howarth has three daughters and has lived in Cornwall for over twenty years.

Also by Lesley Howarth:

Quirx
Welcome to Inner Space

Other titles you might enjoy from
Hodder Children's Books:

Owl Light
Night People
Alien Dawn
Maggie Pearson

Bag of Bones
Helen Cresswell

Spilling the Magic
Stephen Moore

This book is due for return on or before the last date shown below.

3 0 JUN 2000

14 JUL 2000

1 4 JUL 2000

Don Gresswell Ltd., London, N21   Cat. No. 1207   DG 02242/71

a division of Hodder Headline plc

First published in Great Britain in 1998
by Hodder Children's Books

10 9 8 7 6 5 4 3 2 1

A Catalogue record for this book is available from the British Library

ISBN 0 340 69832 2

Typeset by Avon Dataset Ltd, Bidford-on-Avon, Warks

Printed and bound in Great Britain by
Clays Ltd, St. Ives plc

Hodder Children's Books
A division of Hodder Headline plc
338 Euston Road
London NW1 3BH

Contents

BuLLY BoY BADgEr'S LaST BasKet

WE WILL
WE WILL
ROCK YOU

So I'm pulling my suit on again. The crowd's out there roaring like they usually do. The music's blaring out in the auditorium.

WELCOME TO TARMOUTH PALAIS –
YOUR PREMIER BASKETBALL VENUE!

The Pirates'll be on court, warming up. So will the opposition. This is the big one – the semis. The winners get to go to the final. The final's only at Wembley. Chance would be a fine thing.

WE WILL
WE WILL
ROCK YOU

I pull on my badger's body. The leggings. The top.

The gloves. I put on my badger's head and look through my sad badger's eyes. The hat's stuck on to the head so I don't have to worry about it falling off. I just have to worry about looking stupid. Too bad Tarmouth Pirates had to have a *badger* for a mascot. A badger in pirate clothes, it's stupid. A fox, even, would've been better.

I've been Bully Boy Badger for eight months now. *Boy/girl up to fourteen wanted*, the handout said. *Versatile Crowd Entertainer. Able to work well with Cheerleaders.* I don't know about working well with 'em. I don't think they like me very much. *I* don't like me very much. This badger suit, it stinks.

So I chase the cheerleaders around now and then, whenever there's a break in play. I get in their dance-action sometimes and mess up their routines. But I can't do too much of that. I didn't know the suit would be so *heavy*. It's made of this honky nylon fur that's lain in a cupboard a few seasons now, and the smell of it makes me feel sick. Plus it gets really hot and my eyeholes are way back inside my *mouth*, so I have to hold it open to get a good view. At least I get to see every match. At least no one knows who I *am*.

'Good afternoon, *Tarmouth*!' It's Phil in the commentary box. He isn't bad. But no way as good as Scotty. 'Good afternoon, Tarmouth! This after-noon's PREMIER LEAGUE SEMI-FINAL brings you an all-action play-off between Newtown Hawks and your own – your very own – *PIRATES*!'

Major cheering all round. The Pirates aren't doing too badly this season. That's just me under-stating things in case we take a dive. In fact, we've had our best season *ever*. We're doing so drop-dead never-say-die brilliantly so far, I daren't even *think* about it in case it turns to parrot-poo and I wake up and think I dreamed it. Fourth in the National Basketball League, no less, is the best shot we've *ever had* at a top League position.

Today's match is, like, *crucial*. The Hawks or the Pirates go down and no *way* will it be the Pirates, not with Nathan James on the team. We've played the Hawks twice before and they beat us narrowly both times. Technically, we can match them. We've pulled up a lot, this season. The difference is Nathan James. BRAVEHEART, says a banner in the crowd. NATHAN JAMES – WE WIN! I know it, he knows it, the crowd know it. Nathan James *is* the team. There's three or four other key players. But Nathan's our will to *win*.

Nathan James is American – real, not fake. Not like some players who like you to *think* they

3

are, like they have that *cool*, you know, that *finish*. Nathan James has it all. He moves easily under pressure, he's lithe and he's slippy and no one can touch him when he fires from the line and *dunks* that ball in the net. But he isn't selfish, like some players. He'll play the ball or pass it. Whatever's best for the team. He's brave, you know? He's not that big. He's pale and not that muscly. But he gives it all up, every time, and that's what makes him a star. All the kids want their balls signed by Nathan James at the end of the match. They want to get close, to touch him. Watch him shoot a three from the edge of the circle – that's a basket worth three points – he never misses, I'm telling you. If he does, he bounces back or makes that grin. He's good box-office, is Nathan James. Tarmouth Palais *loves* him. And whenever he shoots a hoop, they play his victory song:

NATHAN JONES, YOU BEEN GONE TOO LONG

Phil turns up the heat under the *Mission Impossible* theme and I know he's up in the commentary box, wondering where I am. Usually I'm out in the arena working the crowd by now. Usually I do a few somersaults or pose a bit with some kid. Sometimes I'll shoot a few balls or mess about with the umpires. At half-time I'll do a competition – shoot a hoop, win a ball, that kind of thing. I should be out there now. Today, of all days, I should be out rallying the crowd. It isn't the team, it's me. Somehow, I don't have the heart.

'ARE YOU READY?'

Phil's doing his best. Someone has to work the crowd before the teams come out, but I'm ticked off with Bully Boy Badger, and that's the truth. Maybe it's the suit. Maybe it's because I have a personality problem. Watch their faces when I work the front row – no one *likes* Bully Boy Badger. They pretend they do, but they don't. They hate it when I muss their hair, when I tread on their granny or duff them in the eye or kick their Pepsi down the stairwell, because I can't *see* through my mouth. They think Bully Boy Badger's stupid. They want me to go. They can't stand the smell of the suit. Normally, I don't worry. But a *season* as Least Liked Mascot has to bring *anyone* down.

'ARE-YOU-READY?' Phil turns it up.

'*READY!*' the crowd roars back.

'I – SAID – ARE – YOU – READY?'

'*READY!*'

The crowd sounds monster today. Already we're cooking with gas. They've been here since half past two. But it's a good crowd. The Pirates get good support, and they've repaid it, this season, with their best-ever swing at the Championship. If we can take the Hawks today, we get a shot at Fullerton Raptors. If we take down Fullerton Raptors, we *top the Basketball League*. Top of the League would be full-on *unreal*. I daren't even think about that. It might, for a change, make being Bully Boy Badger worthwhile.

Phil puts on 'Ben Gun'. Dum-dum-*dum*-dum-dum-*dum*-duddle-um. I didn't know 'Ben Gun' before Phil started playing it at matches. Now I know it pretty well. He plays 'Woolly Bully', too, whenever the opposition foul us. Plus he plays the Trumpet Voluntary whenever we're on the attack: Tum! Tiddle-um! Tiddle-um-pum-pum-pum-*pum*-pum-pum-pum! Tum! Tiddle-um! Tiddle-um! Right now he puts on 'Great Balls of Fire' and I have to go. Step out, Mr Unpopular. Mr Dork-in-a-suit. Mr Pay-me-no-money-what-do-I-care. Mr Zero Self-respect. But still I pretend I'm laughing. I could come apart in this suit, and no one would know. Tragic, huh? Tears of a clown, or what?

I make myself leave my broom-cupboard and sneak a look through the double doors. The officials have taken their places. A capacity crowd, like I thought. The cheerleaders – wouldn't you know? – are into their opening routine.

'The Pirettes,' old Phil announces, 'with a full dance programme for *you*.'

The Pirettes are dressed in these *way* short skirts over shiny American Tan tights and cheesy red plastic boots. They're waving their red and green pom-poms – that's the Pirates colours, red and green – and really going for it, like there's some Hollywood agent in the crowd about to sign them up for a lifetime of stardom or something. They're dancing to 'Under Pressure'. Then they dance to 'Firestarter'. I could go in and mess with their routine, except I can't be bothered.

Instead I line up with the Pirates outside their changing-room door. Big Jimmy Grigson tips me the wink. I give him my GO PIRATES neck-throttle. We wrestle a bit and my head comes off. I put it on again really quickly. 'Ready?' says Nathan.

'Ready,' I tell him.

'Let's rip it up,' he says.

It doesn't get any better than this. My chest feels like it'll burst. I'm part of the team for two minutes.

Phil fades out the cheerleaders. 'Thank you — *the Pirettes!*' Then he clears his throat. 'THIS IS A NATIONAL BASKETBALL LEAGUE SEMI-FINAL! WINNER TAKES ALL! TARMOUTH WELCOMES CONTENDERS *NEWTOWN HAWKS!*'

The Hawks run out one by one so Phil can introduce them, which he does really quickly in a bored voice. They *are* the opposition. While the Hawks are busy giving each other five and doing their pre-match routine, the crowd starts to roar for the Pirates. Anticipation builds. We're due out any moment. Our music blares out and fills the hall:

THE THINGS –
YOU DO –
YOU'RE *UNBELIEVABLE!*

This is my big moment. PIRATES ARE GO! As mascot I lead them out, and I *feel* the ripple in the crowd as the Pirates run out after me, all of us smiling and waving like mad, into the whirling red and green lights and the *2001*-type music Phil always plays us in with. We're awesome, no doubt about it. I give it my victory salute – BULLY BOY SAYS WE WIN! – round all four sides of the court, to suss out the Hawks' supporters. They're two or three rows in on the right in the main stand, and they're booing as we come out. Real sporting types, you know? I go into my victory dance anyway, clapping myself, the team, the crowd – hyping it up like anything – while one by one the Pirates take a bow.

'*Little Jimmy Grigson!*' Gimme five. 'Little' Jimmy Grigson's six feet seven. '*Abel "Smash" Howlett!*' Gimme ten. The Smash jumps out like a cracker. '*Waylon "Speedo" Hennings!*' Speedo puts on a spurt and the crowd go wild. Next up are Mickey Hicks and Neil 'The Squeeze' Everett – then, finally, Terry Atcheson. He's dynamite down the centre. One more to come. Phil puts on a fanfare to wind it up:'AND FINALLY – SIMPLY THE BEST – YOUR BOSS AND OURS – WILL YOU GIVE IT UP FOR – *NATHAN JAMES!*'

The crowd give it up *big* time. Nathan James Rules. This is my cue. I'm on court right away, giving the Man my Bully Boy Badger routine for all I'm worth. I hold up Nathan James's hand to the crowd like he's a winner already, which he is. I clap him on the back. I throw a few dummy punches, then I fall flat on the floor when he pretends to punch me back. It's not a difficult job. Nathan plays along. Nathan's the best, I'm telling you.

'*TAKE YOUR PLACES PLEASE!*'

It's time for the game to start. The Hawks win the toss and choose Home End – too bad, but it's not going to throw us. We're up for a quick three-point basket two minutes into time as Terry Atcheson drives up the centre and rings one right away. A burst of 'Simply The Best'. Everyone holds up their PIRATES 3! cards and waves them around like madmen. Nice one, Tel! Way to go! I watch our first score register under HOME on the score panel. Nothing yet for GUESTS. Then I take up my position along the front rows. I pick a few faces to work with. Aggravating the crowd – that's my job.

One face I need to work with as soon as I spot him – and that's not hard with red hair, red face, red sweater – is that stuck-up Jason Payne. The view out of Bully Boy's eyeholes isn't too great, as I said, but it isn't so not-great I could *ever* miss Jason Payne. I hate Jason Payne. He thinks he's so *big*. He once pulled my sister Trish off her bike. Plus he's a dirty liar. Maybe it's not a good time to do the thing I'm planning. Then I decide, so what? Am I going to let *Payne* put me off?

H! A! W! K! S! *HAWKS!* H! A! W! K! S! – do me a favour. Those Hawks supporters are *animals*. Already they've ripped up their programmes and thrown them all over the seats. They hoot during penalty shots. They shout abuse when we substitute. They're totally out of line. They should support a real team. Not a team that cheats.

The action on court's turning nasty. The Cheats – or Hawks – are elbowing Mickey Hicks whenever they think they can, plus they're treading on Nathan James and the umpire doesn't even *see*. Jimmy Grigson shows he's disgusted when the umpire fouls him out when it should've gone the other way, in case you're not *blind*. Everyone hisses and drums their feet while Hawks shooter Tip McMurray takes their two free shots. Two shots. Two misses – *yes*. Phil gives it 'The Laughing Policeman'. *Aha-ha-ha-ha-ha-ha-HA, ho-ho-ho-ho HO.* Phil always plays 'The Laughing Policeman' when the opposition stuff up.

It's my cue to *get* Jason Payne. I forgot to tell

you how easy it is to get away with murder as Bully Boy Badger. As a fluffy old lovable mascot, I can get away with just about anything. I frighten small kids in my smelly old suit, and Mum and Dad still have to smile. I mess up girls' hair with my cruddy old paws, and they just have to laugh it off. I sit in grandmas' laps and they scream with laughter. I throw T-shirts in people's faces, I humiliate them in front of the crowd – but it's only Bully Boy Badger, of course, the mascot you like from a distance.

So I'm making my way towards the centre stand and Jason Payne and his sad band of clueless no-hopers, when suddenly the crowd goes wild. It's a stinging three-point basket out of *nowhere* from Nathan James. Everyone waves their PIRATES 3! cards like crazy. The James boy! Way to go! Phil turns up the victory dance:

NATHAN JONES, YOU BEEN GONE TOO LONG

So what if his name's James, not Jones – everyone sings along. I do my Nathan-James-scores-thing, which is when I dive full-out on the floor in my suit and slide the length of the court. It always goes down really well. I do it every time. Then I get back to Jason Payne. I couldn't have planned it better. This is the perfect time. The perfect day. The perfect Bully Boy moment. See, I'm planning on jacking it in today. Payne is just, like, a bonus.

Payne doesn't see me coming. It's easy to smack off his hat.

'*Hey, Payne,*' I tell him through the hole in my neck, '*check it out.*'

I grab Jason Payne and roll him over. He comes up spitting popcorn. Then he sees it's me – I mean, he *sees* me. Right through my eyeholes. Right through the back of my mouth. Right through my cacky old fur.

'Facey,' he whines, 'let me go.'

My name's Damon Facey, see?

'Payne,' I say, 'in your dreams.'

No *way* have I finished with him yet. I do a whole routine. First I pretend to kiss him. Then I hold up his arms. I pretend I can't live without him. I'm begging him, *please be mine.* The Payne posse laugh like drains. I throw him into my arms and make sure he cops the suit. Old Jason kicks and struggles, but I smother him next to my chest and rub it in. *Bully Boy loves you.* Yeah, right. By the time I let him go, he's limp as a rag.

'It's Facey,' he says. 'Can't you see?' He can't wait to blow the news.

He doesn't get any further. I yank him out of his seat and into the aisle. Everyone laughs as we go. Jason looks like an idiot. He shuts up and plays along. He doesn't have much choice. No way can he be dragged along in front of fifteen hundred people by a giant badger in pirate clothes and still be cool. But still, he wrenches his arm away. 'Bog off, Facey,' he hisses, and tries to hit me.

I dodge and box him back. Then I pretend to fall on him. He isn't enjoying it much.

'Get *off*,' he says furiously. 'Facey, I –'

'Shut it, will you? Oh, *no!*'

Everyone freezes as Hawks hero Tip McMurray nets a flying three-point basket from way outside the circle. The Hawks are on a roll – easy when you tread on the opposition. I check the score-board. *What?* For some reason the Hawks are up 42–29 already. FLY HAWKS! FLY HAWKS! The Hawks supporters go mad. They wave their stupid pom-poms and don't care whose view they block. They've made themselves obnoxious. They're getting up everyone's nose.

'Be back for you later, Payne,' I say. And I drop

him like a doll. 'This is a job for Bully Boy.'

I row-hop up to the Hawks pit as clumsily as possible. I push my way through their seats and I make sure I step on their pom-poms. I pretend to gag the loudest few with my clammy, spammy paws. Then I lie down on the rest and roll around. They have to take it on the chin. It's only Bully Boy, isn't it? After I roll all over them, the Hawks fans go a bit quiet. I climb between them clumsily, knock a few heads together, give them a niff of my suit. Then I get tangled up in their banner. By the time I've sorted it out, the banner's completely rubbished. I make my What-me-worry? Badger shrug. By this time the Pirates fans are loving it. I take a bow. Popular for once. Good old Bully Boy Badger. He never felt *this* good before.

But still we're losing possession. Nathan James looks pale and covered in sweat. They're marking him closely with three big apes, so closely you hardly *see* him. His head is cut. He has to go off. They're actually *shutting him down*. Now we're losing baskets we should be getting. Our defence is *way* not tight enough, plus we're letting them take the game to us, when we should be taking it to them. Thirteen points to make up. *Bad*, but no way impossible. We need the crowd behind us. We have to keep up the pressure.

I front the centre stand and clap my big paws together. *TOGETHER! COME ON, CLAP!* Slowly, the stand gets the message. I put my paws behind my ears – *I'm sorry, I can't hear you* – and the stand claps harder, faster.

PI-RATES – PI-RATES – PI-RATES!

We slow-clap and hiss when the Hawks take a penalty. Phil plays his *Mission Impossible* theme whenever the Hawks make a run, his 'Laughing Policeman' raspberry whenever the Hawks miss a hoop. I kill myself running up and down in my baggy suit. I ruffle hair. I stand on my head. I almost do my *back* in doing back-flips. Suddenly everyone loves me. I know they think I'm a prat, but now I'm a prat with a *purpose*.

EVERYONE CLAPALONG WITH BULLY BOY! COME ON, PIRATES. YOU CAN DO IT!

Slowly we claw back some points. Defence tightens all round. Jimmy Grigson hoovers up rebounds. Atcheson drives 'em up the centre. Abel Howlett slugs 'em in. Nathan James is everywhere, driving, shooting, encouraging, raising everyone's game just by *being* there. We rack up ten points, twenty. You can bet Bully Boy's going wild. But the Hawks slot more in too easily. The scores level up, then we lose it again. We start to lose it badly. Then with twelve seconds to half-time and two points in it, Nathan James does his thing – a heroic, soaring basket which lifts the game just when we needed it, because that's what Nathan James *does*.

NATHAN JONES, YOU BEEN GONE TOO LONG

He gets a standing ovation. The centre stand's this sea of PIRATES 3! cards, as everyone waves 'em like mad. Nathan James's basket puts us *one point* ahead. Then it's half-time. Way to go.

The teams towel off and *strategise*. That's what they say they do, anyway. Nathan James sits down and drenches his head. The coach is talking and slapping his hand. The Pirates bunch up and listen. Situation critical. They're nodding. He's talking and talking and talking. Nathan James gets up and they all join hands, doing that *bonding* thing they do, and I get a twinge when I see them. I'm going to miss them, I really am. But one game can't change a season. Or the way I feel inside.

The Pirettes come out and do this stupid Red Indian dance. Then they dance to the Spice Girls. Then they go off. 'Incredible,' Phil says, when it isn't. 'Thank you – the Pirettes! Now, Bully Boy has something for us. Is it a competition? To win a signed ball? It *is*?'

I do my half-time competition, probably the last one I'll do. Hordes of little kids flood down to try to score a basket. It's a popular competition. I do it every game. You'd be surprised. Sometimes tiny kids win the ball. This time a few try, but fail. Then someone bigger comes down, guess who? It's – no prizes – *Jason Payne*.

'Facey,' he snarls, 'you're so *cute*. Didn't know you liked *dressing up*. We want to see you, right? Either you pull your head off, or *I* will.'

He's about to unmask me, all right. Once I would've freaked. I never told anyone at school. But right now, it's like I'm viewing him at the end of a very long tunnel.

'Payne,' I say, 'do me a favour. You shoot a basket, I'm yours. Fail, and I get to *deck* you.'

'You get to deck me. As if.'

Payne snorts like the pig he is. Then he takes his best shot. He aims, hesitates – it's then that I cough pretty loudly. Payne's ball jumps up, hovers on the lip of the hoop – then bodges out on the edge.

'Shame,' I say, 'too bad.'

'It isn't fair. You coughed.'

'Grow up, Payne, why don't you.'

I swipe his legs from under him as I pick up the ball for the next kid. Paynsie goes down like a sack of cold porridge. He asked for it. I'm not sorry. He picks himself up and goes back to his seat. Moments later, he's spilling his guts. *Know who's inside the dork suit? It's only Damon Facey. Guess who's Bully Boy Badger? No kidding, Damon Facey.* The buzz travels round like a train. It was obvious he's blow it.

'FACEY!' he honks. 'DIG THE SUIT! HEY, FACEY – GIVE US A TWIRL!'

I laugh in my suit. Too much. *Too late, Payne, you lamebrain. I'm quitting, if only you knew it.* He only has a whole *season* to rub it in, and he finds out with minutes to go. It's the end of the road for the smelly suit and the embarrassing pirate outfit. My last game as lovable mascot – Bully Boy Badger's last basket.

I'm tired of it, see? Especially the girls. I can see what they're thinking. *Smelly old Badger,* they're thinking. *Someone does this and thinks it's funny?*

19

Hey, loser. Inside the suit. Are you paid to do this, or have you no life? Being Bully Boy Badger – how sad is that?

Too sad to keep on doing it. They won't even miss me, I bet. It isn't a difficult job. So the victory dive's mine and mine alone, but any other loser could do it. If you don't mind feeling like a freak and seeing the world through your *mouth*, it's really something special. I should know. I've done it long enough.

So half-time winds up with announcements, and then the teams are out. I look at Fred and he nods, and we go into our routine. Fred's a security guard. He stands by the fire exit during the game, but at half-time we do this thing. Fred rushes by me and pops me one as he goes. I shake my fist and rub my head. Then we give it the old comedy-chase routine all around the edge of the arena, me chasing Fred, then me swiping Fred's tie – he wears a clip-on tie, specially – then Fred chasing me to get his tie back, all down the steps and up them, and between everybody's seats. It usually goes pretty well. Breaks the ice after half-time. Sometimes we do something different, but mostly we chase, and old Fred, he loves the limelight. It's the high point of his game. When he goes back and clips on his tie and stands by the exit again, he's pleased with himself, you can tell.

The teams are still warming up, so I badger some kid in Row A. I whip her crisp packet off her, like Bully Boy's *into* crisps. I show everyone the packet. I rub my tummy – yum, yum. Then I tip up my head and drink crisps.

Big mistake. After I finally get the bits of crisps out of my eyes, I hand the kid back her crisp packet. She isn't too amused. Neither am I, to tell the truth. So the second half starts and it all goes our way until Tip McMurray slams in three baskets for the Hawks. I *had* planned not to be needed. But something tells me I am.

Nathan James looks exhausted. He's been on court the whole game. He's made thirty-eight points so far, despite being battered and stepped on. But something's happened since. What's happened is the score. HOME 71, GUESTS 88 – a serious breach of faith. Nathan dips out and sits down. Simon Staples replaces him, and Staples isn't too hot. Nathan James towels his face. Nathan James looks across at me. He's bathed in sweat, white as chalk, and suddenly older than he looks. And suddenly I know. He hasn't got anything left. *Nathan James is all done.*

He beckons me over. He punches my chest. 'Hey, Bully, it's up to you.'

Hey, Bully, it's up to you. I thought it didn't get better than this, but it does. Nathan James lets me know. *He actually thinks I'm a part of the team*, not just some irritating gimmick. Hey, Bully Boy, do your job.

It's up to me to raise the game. Suddenly I know I can. I race up and down. I appeal to the crowd. I whip up a storm in the stands.

THIS IS OUR BIG CHANCE, COME ON! GO, PIRATES! GO, PIRATES! GO, PIRATES, GO!

We get possession, and I kill myself, even over a mean two-point basket. Every point we get, I do my victory-dive. We need every ball we can get – every way to pick up the crowd, to make the fans *believe*. Only the fans can lift the team. And guess who lifts the fans?

Hype it up, Bully Boy, like you never did before. Race around and somersault, and make a fool of yourself. I feel like I'm inspired. The crowd's behind me, I know it. I even field some loose balls into play. I'm Bully Boy Badger, I don't care who knows it. Today I can do anything. Slowly, the fans pick the vibe up. And the team picks it up off the fans. We make one – two – baskets, one after another. Suddenly we're worth 86. I'm almost afraid to check. GUESTS are standing at 94. Suddenly I see we can do it.

WE CAN DO IT! COME ON!

We pull back three points – six. HOME 92, GUESTS 94 – we're back and hanging in there, the scoreboard doesn't lie. I cartwheel up and down. I do the Bully Boy Boogie. I pull out all the stops, and the crowd, they're willing us on and – *yes*! Five fouls for Tip McMurray! Tip McMurray's sent off, as the Hawks start losing it, big time!

Then Mickey Hicks launches this *soaring* ringer from way out beyond the Hawks defence and everyone holds their breath as amazingly, incredibly, and somehow in slow-motion . . .

. . . Will it? Will it? . . . YES, IT WILL –

It arches on into the hoop. Then the arena erupts. 95 – 94, and three minutes left on the clock! It's really one of those moments, what can I tell you? And we don't let up, after that! It's inspired, amazing, beautiful. It's like we're in a different league or something. The Smash nods one in as an afterthought before the defence can recover, and suddenly we're in overdrive. Nothing can stop us now. Jimmy Grigson nets a desperate slam, half falling, half hanging from the hoop, and I hit the deck in my victory dive for the twentieth time since half-time.

HOME 101, GUESTS 94! WE'RE SEVEN POINTS AHEAD! Phil gives it 'We Are The Champions'. *WELL DONE, LADS! GO, PIRATES! GO!*

And we do. We never look back. And when Nathan James takes the line again, somehow the danger's past. Somehow we're twelve points ahead, and we finish the game that way: 108–96. WE WIN! *Our dream ticket to Wembley.* Nathan James falls down and holds his head. He can't believe we've done it, and neither can I. The crowd stand up and applaud him. He gets up and shakes his fist. YES! OKAY! WE DID IT! WE DID IT TOGETHER!

And just as the Hawks slink away and the balloons come down over the arena and Nathan James lifts his tired white face to thank God we pulled it off, I take off my smelly badger's head and make my final bow. *Goodbye and thank you. Signing off. Your first, and maybe your last – your one-and-only, Bully Boy.* I'm about to wave goodbye to it all and run away back to my broom-cupboard, when someone grabs my arms, my legs – when I'm lifted up, somehow.

'Someone raised our game tonight – *A BIG HAND FOR BULLY BOY BADGER!*'

Phil beams down from his commentary box. And the Pirates, they're lifting me up and carrying me round like a champion. They show me off to the crowd. The crowd whoop and clap and go wild. *We did it! We beat Newtown Hawks!* Nathan James hands me up his shirt and pulls on Bully Boy's daggy fur sweater in exchange. I can't believe it's happening. The Pirates are carrying me around like some kind of hero, while Phil turns up the volume on

SIMPLY THE BEST
BETTER THAN ALL THE REST –

And they're shouting my name into the crowd, so *everyone* knows who I am – 'LET'S HEAR IT FOR DAMON FACEY!'

– and I just don't mind at all. In fact, I'm so happy I could burst.

'BULLY BOY BADGER! DAMON FACEY!'

It's one in the eye for Jason Payne. I'm only part of a premier-league team. They're only carrying me round the arena in front of fifteen hundred people. Jason Payne's really gutted. I can see it sticks in his face. And, on top of everything else, *I'm wearing Nathan James's shirt.*

'GIVE IT UP FOR THE BADGER MAN! PIRATES SAY – *DAMON FACEY*!'

So, Payne thought he'd unmask me. Now he knows he can't. I unmasked myself, in a way, but not the way I planned to. *Take a look at the Badger Man, in Nathan James's shirt, no less.* I wave, and he thinks he's something. Jason Payne waves back.

'HEY, FACEY!' he yells. 'WAY TO GO!'

I know he's sick as a parrot. Suffer, Payne, you moron. But I can't waste time on negatives. That's what Nathan James says. Anything not positive's a negative, and we don't have time for those.

Phil plays 'Unbelievable', and I know this time it's for me:

THE THINGS –
YOU DO –

Who cares what Jason Payne thinks? We're Pirates, right? And Pirates stick together. That's what Nathan James says, and that's good enough for me.

YOU'RE *UNBELIEVABLE*

And guess what? *I made the team.* I'm sticking with being the Badger for now. But Nathan says I've got promise. Promise, plus commitment. Nathan's really big on commitment. I'm playing with the junior team, Wednesdays. Some day, who knows, I might wear those red and green colours. You have to believe in yourself. If *you* don't, who will? The view through these eye-holes has changed, no question. I thought that semi-final would be my final game, but it turned out to be my last basket as a sad sack, my first as a *contender*. That was the game Nathan noticed I had it in me. The game that turned me around.

Meanwhile, I'm having the Badger dry-cleaned. I'm perfecting the victory-dive. Fullerton Raptors, here we come.

U.F.O.

'So,' Mr Hatt said, 'what do you think?'

We all groaned — wouldn't you? Design and market a chocolate bar. Some CDT project, right?

'First, think out your approach,' Hatters droned. 'Will the product be fruit or nut-based? What will your chocolate bar's *image* be? Will it be a biscuit bar for the mid-morning snack market, or is it definitely a luxury product? What about texture? Will it be crunchy or creamy? Dark chocolate or light? What about packaging? If you're clear about product profile from the word go, you'll be streets ahead when it comes to design and graphics —'

'Can it be like a Yorkie?' Maxwell Harris asked. 'Sir, can it be like a Yorkie?'

'— so I'm saying think-it-through-from-the-start. Are you with me, Gavin Blatchford?'

'Sir,' Gavin said.

'What am I saying?'

'Um, think about texture.'

'And?'

'It's important to think it through.'

'Yeah, right,' Claire Sales said, '*really* important. What are we, curing cancer?'

'You might not think, Claire Sales, that marketing matters,' Hatters said, in his serious voice, 'but you wouldn't be wearing those shoes or carrying that bag, if it didn't. The lesson economics gives us here, is that . . .'

Mr Hatt droned on about marketing products on the world stage and the importance of a well-designed item, etc., etc. So much for Craft, Design and Technology *that* day. At the end of the lesson he said, 'Right, 9H, Assignment Sheets. I'd advise you to read them through carefully and take it a step at a time.'

Good thing I don't have much work on, I thought. Good thing it won't take ages to do. I couldn't believe it when I saw it:

CDT Spring Term Design Project, 9H

Design and market a chocolate bar, with particular reference to advertising, product profile and cost analysis. Considering your target consumer group and the likely appeal of any packaging, produce a

*complete advertising campaign to include product
research, initial design, prototype packaging,
advertising images/slogans, posters, etc. Assessments
will take into account individual initiative and
public relations/press schemes for launching your
product. Completion date — to be given.*

'This'll take *ages*,' Max Harris moaned. 'Do we *have* to, sir?'

'Not if it's too much trouble,' Mr Hatt said, seriously. 'Take the rest of your life off instead.'

'How will you manage in a design crisis,' Claire asked Max sarcastically, 'if you don't design something pointless in school and think it through from the start?'

'That'll do, I think, Claire,' Mr H. told Claire Sales. 'Cynicism can be useful, up to a point.'

'What point is that, Mr Hatt?'

'The point, Claire, at which it becomes tiresome and counter-productive. What will *your* product be — acid drops, I wonder?'

'It has to be a chocolate bar, doesn't it? That's what the Assignment Sheet says.'

'I'm joking, of course.'

'Of course.'

You don't often see Hatters rattled. Claire

Sales was on top form that day. But it was pointless arguing. We'd have to do the project anyway,
no matter *how* boring it sounded. The funny thing
was, though, it wasn't too boring at all. Everyone
had an opinion about chocolate bars, even, and
including, the olds. Soon as I got home I asked
Mum: ' "*Design and market a chocolate bar, with
particular reference to advertising, product profile and
cost analysis.*" So what do you think?' I asked.

'What do I think about what?'

'*Design and market a chocolate bar, with partic —*'

'Yes, I got that. So what?'

'So how would *you* do it, d'you think?'

Mum thought. 'First, I'd think up a name.'

'Mr Hatt says think up a filling.'

'That just shows how wrong he can be. Take
it from me,' Mum said, 'it's all in the name.'

Mum was right. I started noticing chocolate
bars, after that. I mean, I noticed them *all*, not just
the ones I buy. As well as the usual names, I noticed
Twistas, Spree, Whorl, Snap and Nutz that I hadn't
noticed before. I made a note of them. It's called
market research. That's what I told Mr Tandy in
Le Bon Bon. Le Bon Bon's not French, or anything. It's only the best sweet shop in the High
Street, where everyone goes after school. Mr

Tandy's got big thick eyebrows like Noel Gallagher. Everyone notices them. Soon as I told him about my research, he raised them straight away.

'I have to look at chocolate bars,' I asked.

'You *have* to? That's a new one.'

'Market research,' I told Mr Tandy. Mr Tandy knows me by sight. I'm always in Le Bon Bon for pick'n'mix. 'Market research,' I told him, 'for my project.'

'I've heard a lot of excuses in my time but that one takes the biscuit,' Mr Tandy said.

Le Bon Bon's a cool sweet shop. Mr Tandy knows what he's doing. As well as every kind of chocolate bar, he keeps quality selections for the old dears plus stuff like prawns, brains, shrimps, jellies and cola bottles for people – like me – who're into stuff like that.

'Can I have a quarter of jelly babies?' I said.

'Is this market research, as well?'

'They're just to eat while I'm thinking.'

'Of course,' said Mr Tandy. 'Just to help you think.'

I got out my research file. 'So how many Twistas do you sell? Are Twistas a popular line?' A popular line. It sounded good. I'd picked that up in class.

'I don't know about a popular line,' Mr Tandy said, 'but they go quite well when school turns out on a weekday.'

I made a note in my research file. *Twista*, I wrote. *Sells quite well on weekdays.*

'How about Whorls?'

'The same.'

'And Caramix?'

'Only the toffee flavour. Kids don't like caramel and coffee.'

'And what about image?' I said. 'What kind of people go for Cruisers, would you say?'

'People like me,' said Mr Tandy. 'I like a Cruiser, myself.'

Cruisers. People like Mr Tandy, I wrote. Probably there was a direct marketing link between people with thick eyebrows and chocolate-coated peanut Cruisers (Take Your Time With A Cruiser). It only wanted a bit of research to join the dots. So many chocolate bars, so little time. I'd had no idea it was such a hot subject. It had sounded so *nothing* to begin with.

'Brilliant,' I said. 'You've been a big help. Thanks a lot, Mr Tandy.'

Next CDT lesson, when Mr Hatt asked me to name my Top Three Marketing Priorities, which he did about twenty minutes into the lesson, I brought out my file and said, 'Name. Image. Filling. In that order.'

'Right,' Mr H. said. 'Good thinking. Now we're getting somewhere. Who's done some market research?'

'Me, Mr Hatt.' Gavin Blatchford put up his fat hand. 'I bought sweets before school *three days* this week. I got the wrappers, see?' He brought out a load of them, the pig – Whizzas, Meltdowns, Milkos, Zen Bars, Smoothies, Toppas, Treat, Flamenco, Sin City, Slyders, Double Choc Dark Brazil Twist, the works. Unbelievable. Every chocolate bar you could think of.

'Good – good work.' Hatters didn't know what to say. 'Not *exactly* what I had in mind, Gavin.'

'That's what I *call* market research.' Gavin burped. He looked around, stupid fat toad that he is. 'I just about ate every chocolate bar up the supermarket.'

'Yes,' said Mr H., 'yes, I can see you have. Anyone got any detailed design ideas?'

No one said anything.

'Rita, how about you?'

'Um, I thought about a chocolate bar called OTT – for Over The Top,' Rita Neale said, so quietly you could hardly hear her. Mr Hatt always asks her. He thinks she's good, or something. 'Or I thought about one called The Works.'

'The Works is good,' Max Harris said. 'That's a good name, The Works.'

'Yeah, right,' said Claire Sales. 'I can imagine going into a shop and asking for The Works.'

'Or an OTT,' I said. 'An OTT's all right.'

'It's all right,' Claire said, 'it's not brilliant.'

'What did you think of, then?'

Claire made a face. 'I thought about just, you know, chocolate and stuff. What kind of chocolate people like.'

'You haven't thought of anything, have you?'

'An anxious world waits,' Claire said.

'Don't strain yourself,' Max Harris told her. 'We wouldn't want you bursting a blood-vessel or anything.'

'Not much chance of that,' Claire said. 'What's your idea? Double Choc No Brain? Waste-of-Space wrapped in lush milk chocolate and hazelnuts?'

'Funny,' said Max, 'ha, ha. You should be on telly.'

'I am,' Claire said. 'It's just that you haven't noticed.'

'To-return-to-your-Design-Brief, 9H.' Mr Hatt stood up and rapped his desk. 'I'd like your initial design sketches in by this time next week – is that the bell? What does that *mean*, Gavin Blatchford?'

'End of the lesson, sir.'

'Very funny. I'll ask you again what that *means*.'

'Design sketches in by this time next week,' Gavin mumbled.

'Without fail,' Mr Hatt said.

Almost exactly a week later, 'How about Marx Bars?' Mum said, over the Sunday-evening ironing. 'What do you think? It came to me last night.'

'What did?' I asked her. Not that I cared.

I'd gone all listless and floppy about it, in any case. I was on the point of giving up over CDT and handing in *any* old idea. I was too tired. It was too late. I didn't care, anyway.

'Marx Bars,' Mum said, again.

'You keep saying Marx Bars, what do you *mean*?'

I was getting pretty irritated by this time. It wasn't Mum's fault it had actually got to the *last night* before handing in initial design ideas for CDT. The reason I felt irritated was, I didn't exactly have any. The design cupboard was bare. Any initial ideas had stayed that way. For another reason, I'd done a *major* geography project over the last week and I wasn't about to lose any sleep over Hatters' chocolate-bar scam. That's what I told myself, anyway.

'After the Marx Brothers – you know,' Mum said, 'Groucho, Chico, Harpo and – Zeppo, I think. They made funny films called *Duck Soup* and *Monkey Business*, and Groucho had a big thick moustache and a funny walk. You could have Marx *Bars* with a brand-name *identity*, then have a different filling for each bar, like a Groucho could be dark chocolate with ginger – a bit of a bite – and, I don't know, a Chico could be peanuts –'

'No, Mum,' I said.

'Why not?'

'It's old-fashioned, for one thing. No one would know what it means.'

'No one under thirty, perhaps.'

'That's what I mean,' I said.

Dump, dump, dump – Mum clumped the iron around on Dad's shirt-front as though clubbing the old ironing-board to death would somehow end ironing for ever.

'Like a cup of tea?' she asked, after a moment.

'I'll make it,' I said, and put the kettle on. Then I said, 'I wouldn't mind getting a decent mark for CDT – just for *once*, I mean. I mean, I'm not that bothered. But I wouldn't mind, you know?'

'You'll get there,' Mum said, 'I know you will. It just takes the right idea.'

It just takes the right idea. When I was lying in bed that night, it suddenly came to me. I'd been awake for ages thinking up names for chocolate bars, when I got so I couldn't stop. No *way* could I go to sleep, I'd stayed awake thinking so long. It had seemed amazingly hard to think up names for chocolate bars when I'd tried to think of them in class. Suddenly it seemed so easy. Blitz, Nirvana, Rappa Bar, Lush, Heaven, Choc-U-Like, Luvverly, Droolz, Gorge. I couldn't stop. Every time I tried to turn over and go to sleep a million ideas came crowding in, and they seemed pretty good to me, the way ideas you get in the middle of the night always look good until you think about them next morning. Then suddenly I got this brainstorm. It just popped into my mind. That was the way it happened.

The Unfeasibly Fabulous Object – UFO for short – *ultimate chocolate-bar heaven*. It was brilliant.

Why hadn't I thought of it before? A name that tripped off your tongue, without tying you down to any particular filling. They could have *different* fillings every so often. Why not? That could be a marketing point. Mr H. was keen on marketing points. Plus the ad campaign would be so *easy*. I could see the slogan now: UFO – Out Of This World – the Ultimate Chocolate Experience.

I could see it all so clearly. It wouldn't let me go. I tossed and turned for what seemed like hours, and *still* it came back and *would* make me think it out. Eventually I got out of bed and went downstairs. I tried boring myself to sleep with Dad's paper, but no matter what I read, I couldn't get the Unfeasibly Fabulous Object out of my mind. Every article in the *Evening Herald* that night seemed like it'd been *deliberately designed* to remind me: 'MIND OVER MATTER IN CROP CIRCLE PHENOMENON', 'RECORD CAR SALES OUT OF THIS WORLD', 'CHOCO-LATE PHOBIA DROVE WOMAN WILD'. Even 'CAT IN ROCKET SHOCKER' set me thinking. They even had Readers' Weird Ones too: *Send in Your Weirdest Story and Win Two Tickets to Rumblelow's Unknown Planets – Best Themed Ride in the West!*

Chocolate, rockets, out-of-this-world car sales. Your Weird Stories Featured – could there *be* anything more to remind me? In the end I designed the whole UFO campaign in the middle of the kitchen table at two o'clock in the morning. When I finally went back to bed the whole thing was profiled, imaged, marketed and cost-assessed. Done. That simple. Or not.

Next morning I got up and thought about it. It still looked good to me. I told Dad, on his way out to work, and it looked good to Dad, as well.

'I had a brainstorm last night,' I said. 'UFO – what do you think?'

'What d'you mean –' Dad said, loading his laptop into the car '– have you seen one?'

'I haven't *seen* one. I've *done* one. For CDT.'

'Tell me about it tonight. I haven't time for this now.'

'Yes, you have,' I said. 'All I want to know is, if you saw a chocolate bar called UFO, would you buy one?'

'Depends what was in it,' Dad said.

'But would you take a chance, even if you *didn't* know what was in it? If the wrapper looked good, I mean?'

'Once, maybe,' Dad said. 'I'm sorry. I've got to go.'

I got out my research file over breakfast and wrote, '*Middle-aged male market, impulse buy, once only*,' under UFO – Close Encounters of the Chocolate Kind. Then I packed away my file and ate two bowls of Weetos, straight off. I felt I deserved it, you know? But things were as different, that morning, as if the air'd gone blue or the trees had gone bendy or frogs had dropped out of the sky. It took me a while to realise.

The whole thing stopped being funny, as if it ever was, and started being seriously weird that morning, the morning after I dreamed up – just in time – the Unfeasibly Fabulous Object. I got out my file on the bus to school. I was really pleased with my design, a dark blue wrapper with UFO in *X Files*-type glowing green letters. I'd used my fluorescent marker pen. It looked really good in the dark. If you fancied a UFO bar in the cinema, you'd be able to see to unwrap it; plus, it looked really cool. Mr Hatt, I thought, would be proud of me. I'd thought it through from the start. All the design sketches had the same graphics, like the wrapper, the posters and slogans. It was a really co-ordinated approach, plus I'd thought out some killer marketing points – really professional, I thought. But I wanted some feedback badly. Mum and Dad were no good. They wouldn't know cool if it bit them.

Soon as I got to school I showed Claire Sales my design file. I was pretty safe, showing Claire Sales. Too cool to copy anyone else's work, she was far too lazy, as well.

'UFO.'

'That's right,' I said.

Claire looked at my prototype wrapper.

'The Unfeasibly Fabulous Object,' I explained. 'It's chocolate-coated with three different fillings – you never know which one you'll get. Out Of This World – Beyond Chocolate to Infinity – that's the slogan.'

'How did you think of *that*?' Claire said.

'Why,' I said, 'don't you like it?'

'It's too *good*,' Claire complained. 'What's the matter with you? Hatters'll make me do mine again. Can't you hand in something rubbish?'

It *was* too good. Claire Sales was right. Mr Hatt went mad over my design folder. He practically *ate* my prototype wrapper, he drooled over it so much. Plus he *actually held up my rough sketches* and waved them in front of the class. 'These are what I *call* initial designs,' Hatters raved. 'This kind of work just shows what can be done with a little imagination – Maxwell Harris, are we taking this in?'

So embarrassing. Now everyone would hate me, of course. It's started already, I thought, when no one hardly spoke to me at lunch-time. I couldn't help counting the Twix in the vending machine. It's a funny thing. Once you start noticing chocolate bars, it's hard to make yourself stop.

That night, the sightings began. It all started with Dad.

'You know those UFOs,' Dad said over tea, 'I saw one on my way home –'

'You saw a UFO?'

'– and I meant to get one, but I bumped into Oliver Kitchen – he's looking a lot older these days, his wife's a receptionist at Priory Mount, now –'

'Dad,' I said, 'what are you talking about?'

'These new chocolate bars,' Dad said. 'Aren't they what you were talking about this morning?'

'What new chocolate bars?'

'UFOs. I told you, I meant to get one.'

My whole life flashed before my eyes, I don't mind telling you.

'*You mean, you saw a chocolate bar called a UFO?*'

'Are you having trouble with your hearing? I stopped to get some petrol and I noticed they had those UFOs you were talking about, when I bumped into Oliver –'

'What are they like?'

'I-don't-know-I-didn't-get-one. Poor Olly Kitchen,' Dad said. 'He's almost unrecognisable, he's aged so much since I last –'

'What do they *look* like, I mean?'

'I don't know. Blue and green wrapper –'

'Like *this*?' I opened my file. All my designs spilled out. My sketches, posters, prototype wrapper – in shades of blue and green.

'That's it,' Dad said, 'very nice. Why did you have to draw it?'

'I didn't draw it, I *designed* it. I told you I did, this morning.'

'But you didn't, did you?' Dad said. 'I mean to say, they're real.'

'No, Dad, I made them up. Last night, in fact – ask Mum. We have to design a chocolate bar, and UFO's my idea. We had CDT fourth lesson. Mr Hatt really likes my designs.'

'Have it your way,' Dad said. 'Perhaps you copied it subconsciously.'

'I couldn't have copied *anything*. You must have made a mistake when you were talking to Oliver Kitchen. I made up UFOs – they *don't exist*, all right?'

'I'll get one tomorrow,' Dad said. 'Then you'll see I'm right.'

'I won't, because you're not.'

'I am.'

'You're not.'

'I am.'

'Dad.'

'I know what I saw.'

'Bet you three quid you didn't.'

'Bet you five I did.'

I shook my head. You *sad* man. But, still, it made me think.

Next morning: 'Mum,' I said, 'what's copyright?'

'Copyright.' Mum thought. 'It means something *belongs* to you. Only *you* have the *right* to *copy* it. No one else can take your idea. Like *James and the Giant Peach* is Copyright Roald Dahl.'

'That's what I thought,' I said. 'Dad says I copied my chocolate bar.'

'I wouldn't worry about him,' Mum said. 'He's probably got it all wrong. He can't remember the name of something I've asked him to get at the shops for more than two minutes.'

'But what if somebody steals my idea?'

'I wouldn't show it to Claire Sales,' Mum said. 'That Claire Sales'd think nothing of copying your work.'

'I mean, suppose you invented something, then someone said you hadn't – or someone invented the *same thing* –'

'Oh,' Mum said, 'I see.'

'I mean, how could you prove you thought of it?'

'Well, there's the patents office. Or you could post it to yourself.'

'Post it to *yourself*?'

'That's right,' Mum said. 'You write down your idea, whatever it is, then you post it to yourself in a sealed envelope, then the postmark proves the date you thought of it.'

'Brilliant,' I said. And it was. I went straight up the post office after school. Stuck three of my rough sketches plus a photocopy of my wrapper design in an envelope. Posted it to myself. Simple. Copyright Crabbe Creations, 1997. The post office is next to Le Bon Bon. I thought I'd just slip in.

'Hi, Mr Tandy,' I said.

'Still doing market research?'

'Yes,' I said, 'I am. Got any UFOs?'

Mr Tandy's eyebrows shot up. 'Are you trying to be funny?'

'No,' I said, 'it's a chocolate bar —'

'I've never seen one *in my life*.' His face had gone really white. 'Who's been telling tales?'

'Mr Tandy,' I said, 'I don't know —'

'I hope it's not starting again.'

'What?' I said. 'Mr Tandy, what's not starting again?'

'The old trouble — UFOs.' Mr Tandy brought out his handkerchief and mopped his forehead. He had kind of a Welsh accent. I hadn't noticed before. 'Bringing it right to my face. I thought we'd left all that behind us, when we came here and opened Le Bon Bon.'

'All what, Mr Tandy?' I said. 'I don't know what you mean.'

'Between you and me,' Mr Tandy said, '*never you go admitting it, if you ever see anything strange*. I did, and it ruined my life, *and* my wife Beryl's, as well. It got in all the papers. We had to move house in the end.'

'Why? What happened?' I said. Mr Tandy seemed pretty upset.

'We left the area completely. We had to, see, in the end. You see, I saw a UFO – an Unidentified Flying Object, a space-ship, whatever you want to call it. I saw a UFO once, and *they never let me forget it*.'

'Where did you live before?' I said. I wished I'd never come in.

'Pontypridd,' Mr Tandy said. 'That's where I saw it, see? No one believed me at first. Then everyone thought I was mad. "Seen any funny lights lately?" they said. "Seen any little green men?" '

'I'm sorry,' I said, 'I didn't know. I didn't mean anything.'

'Business dropped off after that, so we moved here and opened Le Bon Bon. It really was a nightmare, I can tell you.'

'People say things they don't mean,' I said, 'it doesn't mean anything –'

'It doesn't matter now.' Mr Tandy put away his handkerchief. 'As long as it doesn't start again. I have to think of Beryl, you see. Now then, what can I do for you?'

'It's just,' I said – I *had* to go on, now I'd started – 'it's just, my dad saw this chocolate bar – *thinks* he saw this chocolate bar – it's supposed to be new out, and it's called the Unfeasibly Fabulous Object, and the wrapper's blue and green, and I wondered if you'd seen it?'

'New one on me,' said Mr Tandy, 'and believe you me, I'd *know*.'

He would, too. I could've kissed him, eyebrows and all. My designs were safe. It *had* to be a mistake. *No one* could launch a new chocolate bar without Mr Tandy knowing about it and stocking it right away. 'Mr Tandy,' I said, 'if you hadn't moved house, you'd never have opened Le Bon Bon. I'm *glad* you moved.'

'Thanks for that,' Mr Tandy said. 'Help yourself to an Ice Pole.'

'Cheers, Mr Tandy,' I said. 'I hope I keep a sweet shop when I grow up.'

'Let me know when you do.' Mr Tandy had cheered up already. 'Cheeky monkey,' he said.

What a rollercoaster ride. What a day. At least Mr Tandy had told me what I needed to know. I felt pretty pleased with myself all the way home. It lasted all of ten minutes. Until I bumped into Maxwell Harris.

'All right?' Max said.

'All right.'

'I told my mum about your stuff last night.'

'My stuff?'

'In CDT. And my mum says you'll catch it when old Hatters sees 'em.'

'Sees what?' I asked wearily.

'Only UFO bars up the newsagent, as if you didn't know. "Look, Mr Hatt,"' Max Harris put on a stupid voice, '"I designed a Wispa and a Crunchie. Aren't I clever?" You can't copy something *real*. What did you think? He wouldn't *notice*?'

Another sighting – or was it? I was starting to feel, well – cross.

'Look,' I said, 'have you *had* a UFO?'

'N-oo,' Max Harris admitted, 'N-oo, I haven't, but Mum has.'

'Did she *say* she had?'

'She *saw* one and next time she's *getting* one, and next time I'm bringing one *in*. Then you can do all your project again because you think you're so *clever*.'

'Thanks, Max,' I said, 'thanks a million.'

To make the end of a perfect day, I saw a bus round the corner. The eighty-nine to Cheap's Place and Chetley Range, to be exact. I kind of noticed the Awayday ad on the side of the bus as I crossed the road. *Let the Train Take the Strain*. Let *something* take it, I thought. Then I looked back at the bus.

It had to be a bad joke. The back end of the number eighty-nine to Cheap's Place and Chetley Range only said:

Beyond Chocolate. Beyond Words. Beyond the Known Snack Universe. New from Haynes – UFO. CLOSE ENCOUNTERS OF THE CHOCOLATE KIND.

Underneath was this giant picture. The designs in my CDT file had spilled out and covered a bus. *My* blue-and-green wrapper. *My* X-Files glowing-green writing. *My* idea. *My* slogan – *my* everything that I'd thought up in bed, and over the kitchen table at two o'clock in the morning – there, like the back end of a bus – *on* the back end of a bus – out of my head and into reality, when I hadn't even *told* anyone except my CDT group and Hatters. This is it, I thought. I've lost the plot *big* time on this one. I really thought I was going mad. I got home and thought, OK. One way or the other, Dad can prove it.

'Well?' I asked him, over tea. 'Did you get one, then?'

'One what?' Dad said, blank as usual.

'A UFO bar, of course. We had a bet on, remember?'

'Oh,' Dad said, '*that*. The funny thing is, I couldn't find one in my usual shop.'

'You couldn't?' I felt — all right. 'Did you go anywhere else?'

'Well,' Dad said, 'I asked everywhere. The filling station didn't have them any more. They said — I don't know — they said they hadn't even had them to *begin* with. I even stopped off at Tandy's. If anyone's heard of them *he* will, I thought.'

'Mr Tandy hasn't got them,' I said, quickly. 'You didn't go in and ask him for a UFO, did you?'

'I did, as a matter of fact. He told me he didn't stock them. He gave me a funny look.'

'So you haven't actually *had* one?'

'Funny-looking eyebrows he's got, that man, I wonder sometimes if he —'

'Dad.'

'All right, all right, you win. I'm beginning to think I dreamed it.'

'I think you saw *something*, all right. Maybe some other chocolate bar.'

'Well,' Dad said, 'it's a mystery.'

'A mystery worth five pounds, I think.'

I'd won, but it didn't end there. *That bus*, I thought. I couldn't stop. *I didn't see that bus*. I just about had myself convinced that UFOs were *my idea* — had been all along — and that for some bizarre reason people kept thinking they saw them, when the number eighty-nine with its CLOSE ENCOUNTERS OF THE CHOCO-LATE KIND poster kept driving into my mind and running down everything I thought I'd got sorted at last. But if Dad was wrong, I could be, too. Supposing *I thought* I'd seen the poster on the bus, because that's what I'd been spacing on all day, but really I saw something else? Or maybe I really *had* subconsciously copied something I'd seen without knowing it. I was sure I hadn't. But it couldn't work both ways. Either I was mad or I wasn't. Either they were real — and no one I knew had actually *had* a UFO — or they weren't.

In the end I couldn't stand it. I had to get it off my chest. Mum and Dad were useless. Next day I rang the paper.

'I've got a Weird One for you,' I said. 'Something for Readers' Stories.'

At least I'd publicise UFO, even if I *was* going

mad. Hadn't Hatters *said* we'd get Brownie points for initiative and publicity? *Assessments will take into account individual initiative and public relations / press schemes for launching your project.* Plus at least it would go on record, no less, that no matter what parallel universe we were in, *I know I thought of it first.*

That's what I said when I rang them. 'I thought you should know, I thought of it first,' I said. 'There's something going on,' I said. 'I want to speak to a reporter.'

One thing the UFO business taught me was that You Never Know. I might even win two tickets to Rumbelow's Unknown Planets, Best Themed Ride in the West. Weirder things have happened. That's what Anita said. The reporter's name was Anita. I told her everything. We had a long talk and a laugh. She had a good sense of humour. She even gave me some tips on how to get into journalism. If I'd known it would be *that* easy, I'd've said something *way* before. 'It makes a good story,' she said. 'You're right,' she said, 'it's weird. Let me get some background and ring you back.'

Anita made a couple of calls, one to a chocolate manufacturer. They asked me to drop in a few things. A photo, one or two drawings. Then I sat back and enjoyed myself. I knew now I wasn't mad. Finally the paper came out, and everyone else knew it, too. Everyone read the article. Mr Hatt even cut it out. He thinks a lot of the school, and the school got a mention, of course. But I think he was, well, proud of *me*. I've never known Hatters so chuffed.

'A commendation,' he announced last CDT lesson, 'for Design, Anticipation of Market Trends and Initiative in Publicising a Product, for excellent work all round and *top marks* for the spring term Design Project.' He shook my hand. His eyes were glowing. 'Well *done*, Alex,' he said.

Then he read out the article. The *Evening Herald* had done me proud. Under a picture of me pulling my designs out of the envelope I'd posted them to myself in – remember? – to prove they were Copyright Me, the article began:

BOUNDARY LANE STUDENT IN 'PSYCHIC' CHOC BAR PUZZLER

'Sightings of a new milk-chocolate phenomenon have had an unexpected effect on a third-year student at Boundary Lane Community College. Alex Crabbe thought she'd seen Haynes' new UFO bar before it was launched – in her Craft, Design and Technology file at school – and she can prove it!

Dubbed the ultimate chocolate experience, Haynes Confectionery had planned the slow release of their new UFO bar at selected shops and supermarkets to test reaction to the new product before the official release date – but not before Alex, thirteen, had dreamed up her own UFO.

'I thought I was going mad,' Alex said. 'We had to design a chocolate bar for a school project, and at first I couldn't think of anything. Then the idea just popped into my head. I stayed up late and drew the designs on Sunday the eighth of March. A day or two later, the sightings began – all my friends said they'd seen a chocolate bar just like the one I designed! I never saw a UFO in my life until Haynes sent me a box of them yesterday – I think I must be psychic!'

The postage date on her detailed designs backs up Alex's story. 'I posted them to myself,' she said. 'I wanted to know how to copyright my idea. Mum says it's just as well I did!'

A spokesman for Haynes Confectionery said: 'This is a remarkable coincidence. Records show that Alex was extremely unlikely to have been exposed to UFO before the night she drew her detailed designs, identical with our original artwork. She had the whole concept to a T. It's incredible to think that Alex may have read our minds. There may be a future for Alex with Haynes – in predicting market developments!'

Now Alex has been awarded full marks at school – for a Design and Technology project so good, it turned out to be real!'

I got a letter from Haynes Confectionery the day after that. Their public-relations department sent me a framed photocopy of the article, and a personal invitation to visit the factory from P. H. Stanley, Regional Director, Haynes Chocolate. I showed it to Mr Tandy.

'Well,' said Mr Tandy, '*we're* coming up in the world.'

'Soon I'll be as famous as you,' I said.

'Me?' said Mr Tandy. 'I'm big in Pontypridd.'

'I didn't mean that,' I said.

'I know,' said Mr Tandy. 'See that you keep

your feet on the ground. Then you can't go wrong,' he said.

I always keep my feet on the ground these days. *Never go admitting it, if you ever see anything strange.* At least I kept Mr Tandy's rule about *one* thing. I never *did* tell Dad I'd seen the poster on the side of the number eighty-nine to Cheap's Place and Chetley Range, when it might have proved he was right all along, when I might've owed *him* five quid. And do you know? I *never saw that bus again*, so I might've half-dreamed it, after all.

And yesterday I finally got to eat one. I undid the wrapper – *my* wrapper. I sank my teeth in (Three Different Fillings – Which Will You En-counter?) and, I have to say, UFO is a pretty cool chocolate bar. Better than anything *I* could dream up. *Beyond chocolate. Beyond words. Beyond the known snack universe.* It was lovely. Out of this World.

The Comfi-Lux

Over 1200 individual pocket springs in a 150-cm (5-ft) mattress. Sumptuous layers of fillings give a truly luxurious sleeping experience, said the label on the mattress.

Sumptuous layers of fillings. A truly luxurious experience. It sounded like a cake. But it wasn't a cake, it was a bed. A giant of a bed. A monster. Her parents' new bed – the Comfi-Lux King Size, to be exact. Lola looked it over with distaste. Its pompous stripped-pine headboard complete with knobs and flourishes – *really* OTT – gave it a cheesy fairytale look, like the bed piled high with mattresses in that story where the Princess can't sleep because there's a pea underneath 'em and she can feel it because she's so *sensitive* or because she's a *princess* or something, which, it went without saying, was much the same thing. Lola sighed. What was that stupid story called? 'The Princess and the Pea.' Obviously.

It had to be the biggest — and the ugliest — bed in the world. The new double bed was a fact of life, whatever Lola thought of it. But whichever way she looked at it, she found she couldn't like it any better. Why had her parents bought it? What were they, *blind*? It looked *smug*, Lola decided. Self-satisfied. A bit of a bully, with its brass-bound corners and its blustering, pompous great bed-head, and the enormous puffed-up *bulk* of it taking up half her parents' bedroom. It wouldn't bully *her*, Lola decided. No way would *she* get used to it in a hurry, big ugly thing. The Comfi-Lux had bossed its way into the house last Friday, but it still seemed like yesterday to Lola. If it thought she was going to accept it, just like *that*, it had better have another think coming.

Hanley's Betta Beds had delivered the giant mistake — the monstrosity, Lola called it — at about half past three the previous Friday afternoon. Lola had just got home from school when the lorry pulled up and they brought it in, piece by king-size piece. Unbelievable. Bed or circus tent — what *was* it? Quilted panels like cliffs came in. Puffed-up bolsters the size of whole grannies or grandads. Polythene-wrapped Formica drawers, in all their hidden beauty.

'I can't believe I'm *seeing* this,' Lola said.

Her mother looked rueful. 'Nor can I.'

More and more king-size pieces came out of the lorry. Lola's heart sank when she saw them. She wanted to shut them out – *no, thanks* – but nothing would stop them nosing in at the door like the prow of a ship or the tip of an iceberg or something.

'It's *huge*.'

'It's big,' Lola's mother agreed.

In came two bulky fold-outs covered in chatty-looking satin. Those two hinged together, worse luck, to make up the king-size bed-base. In came the bed-head – horrible thing. Then the giant mattress – individually sprung, thick as a train and covered in enough polythene to gift-wrap a section of coastline.

'See that?' The Hanley's man showed them the mattress. 'Comfi-Lux – quality label, that.'

Lola stooped to read it. The label on the mattress read: '*The Comfi-Lux – your guarantee of excellence. With more than forty years of bedmaking expertise, quality, comfort and value are assured.*'

They might be assured, Lola thought, but are they worth putting up with *the worst-looking bed in the world*?

'You've got a bargain there, love,' the Hanley's

man had told Lola's mother. 'Quality bed. Do you a lifetime, that one.'

But, oh, it was ugly, Lola thought. Ugly, ugly, ugly. 'Don't you think, Tom?' she asked, long after Hanley's had gone.

'Don't I think, what?' Lola's brother Tom looked in at the door.

'Don't you think it's *ugly*?'

Tom considered the Comfi-Lux. 'I think it's a *bed*,' he said.

Lola considered the Comfi-Lux from every possible angle. At least *she* wouldn't have to sleep on it, with its absurdly informative label, telling everyone how it was made, as if anyone wanted to know: '*Patent comfi pocket springing*,' the label announced. '*Each spring individually pocketed in calico for maximum comfort and support*.'

Big wows. Lola pictured each spring individually pocketed in calico. It was hard, she thought, to find a *single good thing* about the Comfi-Lux. She hated its self-important bed-head. She hated its Formica drawers and the mean little castors *underneath* it. It wasn't even comfortable. You were so high up you felt like you'd fall any minute, so quilted and stifled by it, you couldn't even feel when you'd go. OK, so it wasn't her bed

— but it's ugliness somehow *polluted the house*. How had her parents *liked* it?

'You're ugly,' she'd told the Comfi-Lux, on the day of its arrival. 'You're ugly, and I *hate* you.'

The Comfi-Lux had sat primly on its nasty little castors like an overweight lady in tiny high heels. It *was* what it *was*, and that was that. Some-one had actually bothered *making* it, probably in a factory, probably along with a hundred other ugly beds with lovingly nested springs. It was a *hungry* bed, Lola decided. Not what it seemed at first glance, it was posing as something grand. Posing as something grand, it had an empty space at its core. With an empty space at its core, it was a bed that would gobble you up. And in gobbling you up it would —

'Coming downstairs?' Lola's mother had shouted.

'Not yet! I'm testing the bed!'

— and in gobbling you up, *it would always want more*. It was hungry for people to sleep in it, hungry to shake off its new smell, hungry for someone to *like* it. Lola shivered. Then she slipped down off the bed. You'd crack your head if you fell off the edge. It had to be over a metre to the floor.

'What did you want such a *big* one for?' Lola had asked, downstairs.

'What's it to do with you?'

'It's *horrible*. Why did you buy it?'

'Your father bought it, actually.'

'What is he, *blind*? It's horrendous.'

'Looks comfy, though, doesn't it?' Mum said.

Tom hadn't slept well that night. Finally he'd fallen asleep fitfully, then felt like he hadn't slept at all. He woke up twitchy as a leaf on a twig, ready to drop, but never in the act of falling.

Lola looked ill over breakfast. 'I don't feel well,' she complained.

'Me neither,' Tom said. 'I couldn't sleep. I lay awake for ages.'

'That's what I did,' Lola said. 'I ended up reading a book. Now my neck really aches. I must have slept on it funny.'

'Maybe you need a new bed.' Lola's mother poured the tea. '*I* slept like a rock.'

That'd be right, Lola thought. Buy a bed like a mountain, no wonder you sleep like a rock. 'You'll have to keep your door closed,' she said, 'whenever my friends come upstairs.'

'You what?'

'I mean it,' Lola said, seriously. 'I can't have them seeing the Comfi-Lux monstrosity.'

'Oh. Is the rest of the house all right, or should I redecorate for them?'

That night, Lola felt worse. All evening, everyone else had seemed unbearably irritating – were they doing it *deliberately*? – so that she thought her *head* would burst with the annoyance. By bed-time, thrilling shivers ran up and down her back. She got into bed and the night hours closed in around her. Her body ached, flushed hot, then cold, so finally she put on the light. She felt like running in to Mum, except she wasn't six any more. Finally she dozed off and dreamed of stitching fingers – busy fingers stitching, stitching, stitching little mouths up tight. In the morning she woke up with throbbing ears and little popping lights in the corners of her vision. Her mouth was dry. She felt like she'd woken up on the edge of the world. Feeling more than slightly unreal, she crawled into bed beside her mother. The Comfi-Lux wasn't bad, she thought. It really was pretty comfi.

'You'd better stay right here today.' Lola's mother got up and felt her head. 'You've got a raging temperature. Probably this flu that's going around.'

'I've got it too,' Tom said. 'Go on – feel *my* head.'

Lola's mother felt Tom's head. Then she sent him to school. A long time after Tom had left to catch the school bus, a long time after boiled egg and soldiers and orange juice and paracetamol for breakfast, Lola heard her working. Lola's mother worked from her office downstairs. Tap, tap, tap – Lola heard the word-processor reeling out words that turned, mysteriously, into stories. Nee-bree-ner-ner-ner – the printer churned out the pages. It would churn out pages all morning, and most of the afternoon.

Lola looked through a magazine. There was nothing much in it but fluff and some good-looking faces. She tore a few out. She lay back and thought about Hollywood and Los Angeles, and stars with tasteful-looking beds in languorous white rooms filled with plants, with turquoise pools glinting outside. She sat up and did her nails, feeling a strange reluctance to actually get out of bed whenever she needed more stuff.

In the end, she picked up a book. The book-case in Lola's parents' room held a strange mix of romance, history, rubbish and books that went out with the Ark. They had dull-looking covers and authors with names like Laura Willcox-Harmsworth or Peter Diddley-Squashit or Mabel Dreary-Boredom. But some had magical titles like *King Solomon's Mines* or *The Seven Pillars of Wisdom*. Lola picked out *Beneath the Red Sea*, mainly because of its colour plates of bright but deadly fishes, and climbed back into bed.

She read and read and read. Soon she knew about corals, groupers, anemones and electric eels. Or she *would've*, if she could concentrate, for all the shouting outside. Nicky and Scott next door again. You wouldn't think two boys aged six and four could possibly make so much *noise*. Lola looked at the clock. It *couldn't* be three fifteen. Were Nicky and Scott next door home from school *already*?

Her lunch-tray lay crustily on the floor. Lola binned the cold cheese on toast her mother had brought her what seemed like hours ago. Then she ritualistically ate the chocolate mini-roll, nibbling off the chocolate coating first, then unrolling the sponge and scraping out the filling, then finally eating the sponge. The noise outside got worse. It sounded like balls in a skip or the start of the

Third World War. Lola screwed up her wrapper and stood on the bed. Then she opened the window and settled Nicky and Scott: 'SHUT UP, CAN'T YOU? I'M TRYING TO *READ*!'

Their jaws dropped. They looked up.

'We were only playing horses,' Nicky complained, spreading fingers grey with dirt in explanation.

'Well, play them somewhere else. I'm only ill in bed.'

Nicky stuck his neck out. '*You* play 'em somewhere else. We got *racing* to do.'

Lola gritted her teeth and stuck to her guns. She got through the rest of *Beneath the Red Sea* at lightning speed, despite the sounds of Nicky and Scott jumping up and down on the corrugated iron roof of the shed adjoining the barn next door. She read all that evening, as well. She didn't even go downstairs to watch *EastEnders*.

Her mother brought lasagne up on a tray. Lola read until it had gone cold. Then she ate the corner and ditched the rest. She didn't need food on a tray. She needed to feed her *head*.

That night she had a special dispensation. That's what Dad looked in and called it.

'How are you feeling?' he asked.

'Not too good,' Lola said.

'Not eating much?'

'I'm not hungry.'

'Mum says you like the Comfi-Lux. We'll sleep next door, if you like.'

'No, Dad, it's all right. Really. I'll go back to my own bed tonight.'

But her father wouldn't hear of her moving. 'You're comfy in there – it's a grand bed, isn't it?'

'It's okay, I suppose.'

'You stay right where you are. Special dispensation while you're ill.'

The next day passed, and the next. Feverishly Lola read books in bed, books she didn't even *want* to read. She couldn't stop reading so long as she lay in bed, and so long as the Comfi-Lux had her, she couldn't get out of bed. The hours slipped away in an airless dream and tasted of *Kim* or *The Treasury at Petra* or *Ring of Bright Water* or *Life and Death in the Tower of London*. The Comfi-Lux wouldn't let her go. It wanted more and more. It made Lola read beyond pleasure, comfort or sense. Finally she read in a stupor, faster and faster, and *still* she had to read more. It was making her ill. The Comfi-Lux was insatiable. She didn't care if no one believed her. Three days of insatiable reading and she was *ready* to believe that she lay helplessly under the spell of a king-size bed with a thirst for knowledge as big as its lumbar springing. What did anyone *else* care, so long as she stayed in bed and looked as though she was resting and getting better?

Except that she wasn't. She was getting worse, and Tom saw it. 'Your eyes are red,' her brother noticed, the third day she'd lain in bed. 'Been rubbing soap in 'em, have you?'

'No,' Lola said, 'I've been reading all day.' It was true. Her eyes were killing her. 'Take them away now, can't you?'

She meant her books. Tom pushed them off the bed with his foot. *Kidnapped. British Butterflies. Complete Short Stories of H. G. Wells. Great Steam Ships of the Twentieth Century.*

'Thanks,' Lola said palely. 'I can't start another one now.'

'What — you read all them in *one day*?'

'I can't stop. I *want* to get up and go to school, but the bed won't let me.'

'Yeah, right,' Tom said.

Lola brushed away tears. She couldn't seem to reach Tom through the film enclosing her body. So long as she lay in bed, she couldn't seem to reach *anyone*. She felt like Katy Carr in *What Katy Did* – she'd read it only yesterday – when What Katy Did was break her back on a swing and spend her *life* in bed.

'Tom, I'm not joking,' she said. 'I want to stop, but the bed wants more. It made me read *Pictorial Knowledge* volume four today, as well as everything else. I don't think I can *take* volume five.'

Tom laughed with his mouth, but not with his eyes. He didn't know what to make of it. Something was wrong, but what? He wanted to go – to get away. He didn't want to see. 'How can it be the *bed*?'

'Sit down, then,' Lola coaxed. 'Come on. Come and sit down on the bed, if you don't believe me.'

But Tom wouldn't. 'I'm going out now, all right?' he said. 'I might be back later, OK?'

He *touched* the bed when he picked up her empty dinner tray. But he wouldn't sit down on it, she noticed.

The Comfi-Lux had been made in a hot den of spidery looms and hanging robot arms that screwed up hinges and popped little springs into pockets, Lola knew. The nightmare ran on, hotly, horribly. Each little individual spring squeaked shrilly as the robot arms popped them in pockets. 'Let us out,' they squeaked. 'Don't sew us up in the Comfi-Lux. We'll do anything,' they squeaked, 'only let us go! *Let us out! LET US OUT NOW!*'

Lola jumped up in a sweat. She ran out of bed to the toilet, then she ran back really fast. But it was too late. The Comfi-Lux sensed her presence. Of course, it knew she was awake. *Switch on the light*, the bed said. Lola switched on the light. *Pick up a book*, the bed said. Lola picked up a book. *Start reading, then*. Lola started. She read until three in the morning, red-eyed, reluctant, half dropping-off, half not. *Sit up*, said the bed, *we're not finished*.

'I am!' cried Lola. *You're not*. 'Read 'em yourself!' Lola cried. 'I can't go on! I don't *want* to read *Pictorial Knowledge*! Or *Brighton Rock*! Or *Kim*! Or the *Encyclopaedia of Rocks and Minerals*, or a *History of the Old West* – got it?'

Suddenly Lola felt as if the weight of all the world's books were standing on her shoulders. *Pictorial Knowledge*, volume five, slid heavily on to the floor. She wouldn't read any more tonight, not if the Comfi-Lux nagged her to death or smothered her slowly in a Luxurious Sleeping Experience, not if – *the bed ate her up*. Each of the individually pocketed springs inside the Comfi-Lux sighed a little as Lola lay back, exhausted.

She didn't sleep very well. By seven thirty in the morning when her mother looked in, felt her head, and went out again, Lola had thrown her arms and legs into a hundred feverish positions over most of the *not* Comfi-Lux. She tossed and turned uncomfortably – the bed seemed to be made of something unbearably knobbly, like pebbles or other people's heads – until Tom loomed in at eight o'clock.

'Oh,' she said, 'what is it?'

'You,' Tom said, 'that's what. What was all that shouting about last night?'

Lola sat up painfully. 'There was something under the mattress. I didn't sleep very well.'

'Mum says she's getting the doctor.'

'Oh?'

Tom nodded. 'Mum says, enough's enough. She's ringing the health centre now.'

'Can you look under the mattress?'

'Under the mattress? Are you kidding?'

'There's something *awful* under it.'

'There's nothing,' Tom said, 'you're mad.'

'It's the bed,' Lola wailed. 'It's punishing me.'

'It's *punishing* you? What for?'

'I didn't read enough last night – we only did volume five last night, when we ought to have finished volume six.'

'We?' Tom asked. 'Who's *we*?'

'I. Me. The Comfi-Lux.'

Tom smiled. He tried to make it look natural. 'Well. Got to go. See what the doctor says.'

'See what the doctor says about what?'

'You,' Tom said, 'you know you're *seriously* –'

'What's that over there on the floor?' Lola flapped her arm impatiently. 'Over there, by the door – can't you *see*?'

Tom picked it up. A hard, dry, grey-green *pea*. 'It's – a pea,' he said.

'I knew it.' Lola fell back in the bed.

'It's only a pea,' Tom said. 'It must've come out of something.'

'Bring it here,' Lola ordered.

Tom brought it.

'I *told* you there was something under the mattress.' Lola examined the pea. 'No *wonder* I couldn't sleep.'

'Why would there be a pea under the mattress?' Tom asked. Why *would* there?

'To test me, of course. I told you.'

'To test you. Right. Of course.'

The Comfi-Lux

Tom backed out. He looked at Lola, deep in the monster-sized bed. Her small head looked lost against its pompous-looking headboard. The Comfi-Lux seemed to enclose her. Soon it would gobble her up completely. He'd come home from school and there'd be nothing left of Lola except a pile of books, a half-drunk drink of Lucozade and a – pea. And that would be all. *And the Comfi-Lux would have won.* Tom shuddered. It was only a bed – an ugly bed. A bed with a big personality. And not a nice one, at that.

Lola had closed her eyes. She hadn't even noticed he'd gone.

Tom cleared his throat. 'Yes. Well. I'm going now.'

'Uh-huh.' Was that a goodbye?

'Smell you later,' Tom added.

'Not-if-I-smell-you-first.'

The voice was deep, almost pompous. It didn't, Tom thought, even *sound* like Lola any more.

'Can you tell those kids to shut up?'

'What – Nicky and Scott next door?'

'They're getting on my nerves, all right? Plus I need a drink.'

'Get me this. Get me that. Get it yourself,'

Tom said. 'What are you, the Queen or something?'

'I have to ask you, don't I? If I can't do things myself.'

Lola had lain for a week in the Comfi-Lux now. The changes were obvious to everyone. Her voice was low and weak, her tone imperious and demanding, her eyes dull, her skin-tone duller, her parents increasingly anxious. Words like *glandular fever* were being bandied about. Until Doctor Inman called, that is. Doctor Inman brought a new word with him. The word he brought was *malingerer*. Lola hadn't heard it, so she didn't really know. She hadn't even asked what Doctor Inman said. She didn't know a malingerer was someone who pretended to be ill when they weren't ill any longer. She didn't know Dr Inman had prescribed fresh air, activity and school on Monday. She wasn't even curious. She didn't care what he – or anybody – said.

'Look at this,' Tom said.

'What?'

'It's about eccentric people.'

'What is?'

'This article in *TV Quick*. Brian Wilson, musician, stayed in bed *three years*, it says here. Became enormously fat.'

'Why did he do that?'

'I don't know, he just did. That's what'll happen to you, if you don't watch out. There's more. Eccentric millionaire Howard Hughes –'

'I don't care, I'll do what I like!'

'And everyone else gets to *let* you? Run the world from your *bed*, why don't you?'

'Well, I'm doing okay.'

'No,' Tom said, 'you're not – you're doing rubbish. You're making everyone wait on you hand and foot. But not me – as from now.'

'Shut the door on your way out,' Lola ordered weakly.

'I might,' Tom said, 'or you might have to shut it for me.'

Lola struggled upright. 'SHUT THE DOOR!' she yelled.

'You're scary, you know that?' Tom said.

But it wasn't really Lola, Tom thought, the miserable Hitler in bed. She wasn't like she normally was, so long as she was in it. How could he get her *out* of it? Would she really get up on Monday, like Doctor Inman said? It wasn't really Lola who was scary. *The really scary thing was that bed.*

'Getting up day,' Tom announced in Lola's ear on

Monday. 'Come on, shift it. Let's go.'

'Leave me alone, I said.' Lola buried her face in the clean white deeps of the Comfi-Lux. Tom stripped the duvet back. How small she looked. How frail. Like a small white sail on the ocean.

'Mum says get up or get hungry.'

'What?'

'You heard,' Tom said. 'There's nothing wrong with you.'

'That's not what Mum said.'

'It's what Dr Inman told her.'

'It isn't.'

'It *is*. Shall I get her?' Tom took a deep breath. 'Mum – Mum! Come here!'

Lola's mother pounded upstairs.

'What is it? Has something happened?'

'She won't get up,' Tom said.

'I really don't feel like it, Mum.' Lola's voice fell an octave or two. 'I don't really think I'm up to it, do you? I mean, I wouldn't want to collapse in school. I wouldn't want them to think you'd sent me in when I wasn't well. They might not think it appropriate.'

'Appropriate?' Lola's mother stared. 'I don't know why you're talking like this, Lola. Dr Inman said you can go back to school any time you're ready.'

'But I'm *not* ready, do you see?'

Lola's mother looked at Tom. Tom swallowed. 'I think,' he said, 'she ought to get out of bed.'

'I agree. You've had a fever. You're feeling weak. How can you tell how you feel if you never get up?'

'I *do* get up. I acquire knowledge. I have individually pocketed springs.'

'Lola! This isn't funny!' Lola's mother felt frightened, she didn't know why. 'I want you up and about today. Mr Snell sent you some homework. You can work on the kitchen table, then tomorrow you go back to school.'

'Tomorrow,' Lola echoed.

'You can keep that silly voice for telling jokes. One more day,' her mother warned.

'One more day,' Lola echoed.

'I mean it.'

'You mean it. I understand.'

'Just so long as you do.'

Lola seemed strangely unlike herself. Her mother withdrew with the feeling that what she had said hadn't sunk in at all.

The day passed as other days had. Lola knew it was serious. She didn't even read. Instead, she lay in a light dream and thought about headboards and rivets, factory-finishing and superior springing of the type she knew she had. She thought her mother came in – and nagged her and flung down some of her clothes. Lunch downstairs, her mother had said, *when* you're prepared to come down. But lunchtime came and went, and Lola didn't go down. Nicky and Scott came home from school and took up howling outside. Lola listened. It didn't seem fair. They had such *life* outside.

The front door slammed downstairs and her brother Tom came home from school and *still* Lola hadn't got up. Tom pounded straight upstairs. She could see the displeasure in his face. 'I thought you were getting *up* today.'

'Tom – please –'

'I told 'em you're throwing a sicky at school. You've got *loads* of stuff to catch up.'

'You don't understand, I can't just –'

'What's *happening* to you?' Tom demanded. 'You're turning into this huge great bloater who knows everything in the world and never goes out. What's the point of *that*?'

'The biggest,' Lola said faintly, 'and the best – that's what it's about.'

'Biggest and best – like the bed, you mean? You're turning *into* that bed.'

'That's so stupid — you're sick.'

'Why don't you ever get *out* of it, then?'

'I'm going to school tomorrow, Mum said.'

'Good job,' Tom finished. 'That bed's got it over on you. You need to get legs and a *brain*.'

Tom shut the door and went out.

'Tom — please — wait!' Lola called him back. Nicky and Scott's shouts had dwindled away next door. This was, very possibly, the end. 'Tom! Please! Help me!'

'What did you say?' Tom put his head round the door.

Lola struggled to repeat it. But her voice had sunk pompously low. 'I need an adjustment — HELP — twelve hundred pocket springs — ME — give truly luxurious support —'

'Yeah, right.' Tom slammed out, disgusted.

'TOM!' Please come back, Lola thought. 'TOM!' *Please.* 'TOM!'

'*What?*' Tom's head reappeared at last.

'Tom — please — my very last chance —'

Lola put a foot out of bed. It took all her strength to do it. She reached out to Tom with both arms. 'Tom,' she said, 'please help me.'

Tom was at her side in a moment. 'I want to,' he said. 'How?'

'Pull – pull me out of bed a bit, first.'

Tom pulled. 'What else?' he said, urgently. 'Tell me.'

'Nicky and Scott,' Lola whispered. Her voice was her own, at least. 'Please, Tom. *Get Nicky and Scott.*'

'They're noisy. Why would you want them?'

'Just get them. Please.' Lola whispered.

'What on *earth* – ?'

Lola's mother opened her bedroom door and took in the scene open-mouthed. Nicky and Scott from next door. Bouncing around on the brand-new Comfi-Lux bed! And Tom! And Lola! Making so much noise they couldn't *hear*.

'Yay!' Nicky screamed. 'I got to *bomb* 'em! I bomb-bomb-bomb –'

'I bomb you *back*!' Scott boffed his brother with pillows, again and again. 'An' I *get* you I do –'

'An' I get you –'

'*Oh, no! Mars attack!*' Nicky pointed at Tom, bouncing hugely behind Lola, already armed with a pillow. 'Red alert! Bounce 'em off! Bounce 'em – go on – *bounce* 'em –'

Nicky and Scott upped their bouncing, and for a moment it was touch and go who would bounce *who* off the bed. Tom and Lola weighed in with their pillows, but Nicky and Scott had a good rhythm going already. Nicky bounced mightily, peaking just as he spotted Lola's mother open-mouthed at the door.

'Nicky and Scott! Tom and Lola! Can you get down off the bed?'

The Comfi-Lux sighed with relief. Its head-board banged against the wall as Lola bounded off it. Lola's mother looked at her. Her cheeks were flushed, her eyes bright. She looked, well, so much *better*. Like the little girl she'd once been. Little and bright and shining.

'I don't know *what* you all think you're doing.' Lola's mother tried to look stern.

Nicky and Scott climbed down. Tom put the pillows back.

'Please, Mum,' Lola said, 'we're only playing Mars Attack.'

'Not on the Comfi-Lux, you're not. Lola, I'm surprised.'

'So'm I,' Lola admitted. 'But it's broken the spell, don't you see?'

'Spell? What spell?'

Lola's mother looked from Nicky and Scott, to Tom and Lola – flushed, panting, giving out rude health like anything. *What a change*, she thought. *How like herself Lola looks. How well. How full of life.* Suddenly Lola's mother realised just how pale and how ill – how *bed-ridden* – her daughter had been. Looking at her now – eyes shining, playing with Nicky and Scott as though she were six years old – it was difficult to remember the world-weary invalid of yesterday or this morning. Even the sick-room *air* had lifted. And Tom – Tom, especially, looked pleased and flushed, as though he'd done something clever. They *all* looked pleased and flushed – all except the Comfi-Lux, which looked rumpled and out of sorts. It had lost its dignity, all right. *Perhaps it had needed to.*

'*What* spell?' Lola's mother repeated, knowing, in the moment she said it, exactly what spell it was.

'Oh, *you* know,' Lola said. 'I wasn't so good, was I? But now I'm bouncing, I'm better, *if* you know what I mean.'

'Now you're bouncing you're better.'

Tom cleared his throat. 'She's right,' he said. 'Don't you think she looks great?'

'She *does* look great,' Lola's mother admitted.

'I feel great,' Lola said.

'And we did bouncing, all right,' Nicky said, twisting his fingers.

'An' it's a *horrible* bed an' we *biffed* it,' his brother Scott added.

'Thanks very much,' Lola's mother said. 'Let's hope you haven't biffed it too much.'

'It's just – the Comfi-Lux needed sorting,' Lola explained in a rush, 'and we've sort of *broken it in*, you know? And now it's like any *other* bed, only bigger and better, of course, and I knew they could do it – Nicky and Scott, I mean – and I had to ask Tom to get them and then we bounced the newness away, and all that – and it was getting above itself you see, and it wouldn't let me get up – and now I feel *brilliant* – don't I, Tom? – and I think I'll get up and run a bath.'

The Comfi-Lux sat squarely on its dented little legs while Lola ran on and on. It was a broken bed. There was no obvious damage. Its newness – its *uniqueness* – gone, it was just a rather ugly king-size bed. Its twelve hundred individually pocketed springs still nested cosily inside its sumptuously layered mattress. Its headboard wasn't really damaged. Comfort, Quality and Value were still Assured. But the spell was truly broken. It would never be the same bed again.

'And tomorrow I've got PE so I need my sports shirt clean, plus my geography file needs sorting for Mr Reeve and I'll have to ring Josephine Naylor to find out what maths we're doing.'

Bursting with health and energy, so full of life she was practically walking up walls, she'd probably stay up all evening, and practically half the night. Tom and his mother watched Lola gabble on. She had so much to say, it seemed she would never stop.

The Undersea World of Michael Finlay

The stamp on the envelope said *Avalon Water Services Limited*. Michael Finlay picked the letter up off the mat. *To the Occupier*, it said on the front. He was an Occupier, wasn't he? Michael opened it swiftly and read:

> *Notice of Interruption to Water Supplies. It is proposed to re-line the water mains in your area. Your water supply will be interrupted on the following days. Temporary supplies will be available from bowsers placed in your area.*

Bowsers? What were *bowsers* on a good day? Michael Finlay frowned. 'Mum,' he said, 'they're going to dig up the road. Come and take a look at this.'

The day the men came to dig up the road, Michael Finlay took no notice. He walked past the water men to the bus stop and hardly

87

registered the picks and sandbags, traffic cones, fencing, manhole covers and JCB at all. ROAD CLOSED. RESIDENTS ONLY, said the sign at the top of the road. Much more exciting was the sign introducing the holes – four large holes – which soon appeared in the road that wound down to the sewage works, where the water men had their headquarters. CAUTION, said the sign introducing the holes. MULTIPLE EXCAVA-TIONS AHEAD.

Multiple Excavations Ahead. It sounded a bit revolting – or was that evacuations? Good job they were down at the sewage works, Michael Finlay thought. Probably the best place for 'em. Whatever Michael Finlay thought, the Multiple Excavations went ahead. So did the JCB and the snaking nylon hoses which dropped their heavy heads into the holes and sucked out rusty water.

What, exactly, was going on? In the end Michael Finlay took the trouble to ask. 'What are you doing, exactly?' he asked the Avalon Services man.

'Cleaning the water pipes out and re-lining the sides of 'em with plastic.'

'Oh.' Michael digested this. Then he said, 'But how can you see down the pipes?'

'We put down an optic-fibre camera. Then we put down a scraper to scrape the scale out. Then we pump down two different plastics plus a spinning head powered by air under pressure to plaster the pipes with plastic as it goes. Clear?'

'Clear.' Michael Finlay nodded. Then he wondered what the man had said.

Michael Finlay soon got bored with it all. Day after day the men fussed around pumping messes out of the holes they'd dug and clunking around with pipe junctions and manoeuvring their JCB and making everyone who tried to pull into Michael's road ever so slightly cross. He got used to having to walk up the road a bit to meet the school bus, because the school bus, like a large lady, couldn't turn on a sixpence, which was about all the room the water men had left between their holes in the road. He soon got used to the bowsers, which were nothing more than white plastic tanks filled with water you could use when the taps ran dry, which they did whenever the water men wanted to do something particularly tricky like joining up two big throbbing mains with a clunky brass junction, which they wanted to do quite a lot. The notice on the bowsers said: 'Water Mains Rehabilitation Temporary Water Supply. A. W.S.L

Bowsers – Boil Water For One Minute Before Drinking.'

Michael's mother boiled tap-water for one minute for quite a long time before she realised it only meant the bowsers, as Michael explained.

Michael said, 'It only means the bowsers.'

'What does?' Michael Finlay's mother set a pan of water on the cooker.

'The boil-your-water notice. It doesn't mean we boil *ours*.'

'Are you sure?'

'I'm sure – can't you see? It says, on the side of the bowser.'

'He's right,' Michael's brother Stuart chipped in. 'We just need to run it if it's cloudy.'

'I thought they meant boil *all* the water.' Michael's mother sighed. 'Well, I wish they'd get on and *finish*.'

But the water men seemed far from finishing. Every day the holes in the road seemed more like permanent fixtures. Every day Michael Finlay passed them without a moment's thought, except for one day when he took a peek inside one on his languid way home from school. Deep in the hole by the bus stop, a brass-headed pipe like a snake pulsed under layers of slate descending to oily-looking depths. The layers of slate looked like hanks of carbon paper or the leaves of thin grey books, one on top of another, going down for ever and ever. It was funny, Michael thought, what the road looked like underneath the everyday road that you knew. It didn't look like you thought it would. It looked like nothing on earth.

And the water men dug and their snaky pumps pumped, and Michael Finlay came and went to the school bus stop past them, and thought no more about it until the water blurted cloudily out of the taps or his mother grumbled that there wasn't any. And the holes in the road became commonplace and Michael Finlay hardly noticed them – until the day of the Talk.

The Talk had been advertised all over the village.

'I don't want to go,' Michael Finlay told his mother.

'Yes, you do,' his mother said. 'It'll be interesting, you'll see.'

'No, it won't. I won't like it, Mum, and I don't want to go.'

'It'll help you no end with your geography. You won't have to do so much reading.'

Michael Finlay weighed this idea against a

strong inclination not to go. But that was how he ended up sitting in the front row of a talk entitled 'One Hundred Million Years of Local Geology – A History of the Cap River Valley'.

'It'll be *boring*,' Michael grumbled on the way there.

But it wasn't. The Talk on local geology wasn't boring at all. It was more than interesting. It was fascinating. Michael Finlay forgot the time. He forgot his sweaty socks and his unyielding chair and the head of the person in front. He forgot everything except the slides of shifting landmasses, of shells and shingles and mud-flats, magically changed into clifftops. He even forgot to be hungry or thirsty or bored, as the Talk ran on. Everything came and went, he saw, in chunks of time divided, like lottery wins, by very many noughts. Rivers waxed and waned. Mountains rose and fell. Especially in the Devonian Period, when red sand had slid off the mountains and heaped up in cliffs by the sea. Except that the sea had been nowhere near at the time. Seas – and continents – moved around all the time, it seemed. Michael could hardly keep track of them.

In the Devonian Period, Britain had been no more than an interestingly shaped bump on a supercontinent way below the equator. Then, slyly, it had moved up. Volcanoes had heaved and erupted and thrown up rocks the size of cars. Then they'd melted into granite and sat, like a tray, under ancient deep seas filled with fishes that lived and died and evolved and became extinct before anybody ever even *saw* them. Michael watched the slides flicker up, slides of cliffs and rocks and landshapes nearly, but not quite, like the land-shapes he knew so well. This was a world strangely distorted, unlike anything he knew or had tried to imagine, a deep-sea world of unformed fishes and coastlines nowhere near where coastlines ought to be. Plus the village – the village *hall* – used to be under a *sea*.

It was a sea! Michael rehearsed it to himself. The valley in which he'd lived for half his life had been under a deep, deep sea for, like, the longest time. *It was a sea!* He said it over and over. It was a *sea*, and everything around him once swam under fathoms of water filled with fishes no one knew, and the hills and the valleys and the rocks and outcrops and lanes *were just what the deep sea had left*. It was pretty hard to believe it, but it was true. Michael Finlay's brain buzzed. Everything – the hedges, roads, the holes in the road – looked different on the way home.

He tried to tell his father when they got back. 'There's corals and mud, way down – and it's the mud we're *living* on, see?'

'Hold on, what mud?'

Suddenly Michael knew what mud. 'I've seen it, right? You know those holes in the road? If you look down them, right, there's, like, layers and layers of slate, going right down to the bottom. And if you could look under *that*, there'd be a thousand feet of mud –'

'*A thousand feet of mud?*'

'That's right, and the mud got squashed into rock, and that's what all the slate is. And we're just all living on mud. Right at the bottom of a sea.'

'Fascinating, isn't it?' Michael's mother said. 'I told him he'd like it if he went.'

'He didn't fall asleep, then.' Michael's father winked. 'He usually does, old Mickey Finn. You have to nudge him now and then, else he starts to snore.'

'Yeah, right,' Michael said. 'As if.'

Michael Finlay's father called him Mickey Finn sometimes, just because of the school play, where he *once* fell asleep when he was four. A Mickey Finn was a drink that made you sleep.

They slipped each other Mickey Finns in old gangster films. Usually some woman with tightly rolled hair would open a ring filled with powder and tap it into a drink and pretend she hadn't. Then whoever drank the drink would fall down shortly after they drank it. Michael Finlay fell asleep after drinking squash at the school play, so his dad called him Mickey Finn. Also it sounded like his name. It wasn't really funny. It wasn't really anything, except a silly joke.

'The holes in the road'll be going soon, anyway,' Michael's father said.

'No kidding,' Michael's brother said. 'I thought they were leaving them there.'

'They've got to wrap it up by the twenty-eighth. I spoke to the boss last night. They're putting a pig in tomorrow.'

'A pig? Where?'

'Down the pipes. They have to re-line them with plastic.'

'That's cruel,' Michael said. 'How can they put a *pig* down the pipes? It'll only get stuck or something.'

'It's *called* a pig,' his father explained. 'It's a machine they put in which coats the pipe as it goes.'

'Oh,' Michael said, 'that air-pressure thing. It isn't called a pig.'

'It can be,' Michael's dad said.

'So long as it isn't real.'

'Yeah,' Stuart said. 'It *is* real, as it goes. What d'you think that lump under the bus stop is? Only the pig they put down the last time they came.'

Next day Michael Finlay looked at the holes in the road with new eyes. How could he not have read it before? The layers of slate in the hole in the road by the bus stop were the leaves of a very ancient book. Each wafer-thin layer represented, probably, a season's deposit of mud, and underneath his feet lay *a thousand feet of mud*. How many seasons was *that*? The mud had built up, layer by slimy layer, in a warm deep sea that had washed the sides of rising granite hills – like Cap Hill, which stood over the valley – forced upwards by the great mountain-building stresses of the Devonian Period. Michael Finlay grinned. He could practically give a Talk himself. He'd better book the hall.

Soon as he got home from school that night he booted up the CD ROM Encyclopaedia and made it search for DEVONIAN. It took a minute or two, but there it was:

Devonian Period, fourth division of the Paleozoic era of the geologic time scale, spanning an interval from about 395 million years ago to 345 million years ago, and named for Devonshire, England, where the rocks of that period were first studied in the 1830s.

That had the Devonian just about nailed – but what about warm, deep seas? Michael Finlay read on:

During the Devonian period of mountain-building . . . the stable platform of the continental interior was occupied intermittently by warm seas in which reefs of coral and sponge grew.

In which reefs of coral and sponge grew. That'd be right. Michael sat back, excited. They'd said at the Talk there'd been corals and sponges. Coral and sponges in the slates, probably, down in the hole in the road. How strange to think of deep-sea things, swimming where he now stood. How weird it all was – how mixed up with water, somehow. It was funny the way the water men had arrived to dig holes in the road, just when he'd been to a Talk which made him realise what was *in* them.

Michael watched the water running out of the tap as he cleaned his teeth that night. The very same water, he thought, might've run in that warm, deep sea. The water that came out of the tap – well, it just went round for ever. Columbus had sailed on it. Shakespeare had drunk it and – well, Shakespeare had drunk it. And people had been going to the toilet for a very long time indeed. Yuk. But there was only so much water. And it had to go round and round. Up into rain off the sea. Down over the land into rivers. Through humans and animals. Round and round and round. In ancient seas, in modern seas, it didn't really matter. It was all the same, whether the water came out of taps through newly re-lined pipes, or out of Tudor rain-barrels or an oasis under a date palm, if it dripped off some tropical leaf or soaked away in a paddy. Round and round and round. There was only so much water. Michael considered his toothbrush. The water sluicing it might *just* have been ancient sea. He swam down the corridor to bed. He actually *felt* like he was swimming. Swimming through hidden deeps.

He looked up DEEPS next morning. There were several horrendous troughs in the sea-bed where cities the size of New York could get lost like a coin down the sofa. The Challenger Deep off the Philippines plunged some thirty-five thousand feet below the surface of the Pacific, where nameless blind fishes bulged under un-imaginable pressures. Michael Finlay read on. He went to the library and got out books. He put up pictures of fishes. He brought rocks into his room. He drew the curtains and sat in the dark, the darkness of undersea deeps. He swam in and out of the kitchen for food and swam away from anyone who bugged him. Two weeks passed in the undersea world. One night he wet the bed. He was frightened, he didn't know why.

He swam into the kitchen next morning.

'What are you *on*?' Stuart asked. 'Why are you always doing that stupid *swimming* around the house?'

'I'm just, like, imagining we're under the sea.' Michael got out a cereal bowl. 'Nothing *wrong* with that, is there?'

'Fine.' Stuart shrugged. 'Carry on. Don't mind me if I space-walk.'

Michael didn't. He didn't mind anything else, all day at school, but the wash of the seas in his ears. They washed over maths with Miss Cardew, they washed over French and RE, they washed over English language with Arnold Rames.

'Michael Finlay, can-you-hear-me?' Mr Rames had said. 'Could-I-ask-you-for-your-attention? If it's not too much *trouble*, that is.'

'I've got a cold in my head, Mr Rames.' His own voice sounded submerged to Michael Finlay. 'I can't hear very well.'

'Cold in the head or not,' said Mr Rames, 'can you give me a split infinitive?'

Swish and *swash*, the seas played in Michael's ear like the sound of distant breakers in a seashell. Split infinitives faded in his imagination against the strange and mysterious creatures he heard sporting in that surf. 'Um,' he said, 'I –'

'Yes?' Arnold Rames tapped his desk.

'To boldly go?'

'Correct.'

'To swiftly rise. To sadly fall.'

'Ah, yes.'

'To violently erupt, to quickly flood, to desperately drown.'

'Quite.'

'To slowly sink. To softly bury. To coldly die.'

'Thank you, Michael. That will do. I think you should see the doctor about your ears.'

The Undersea World of Michael Finlay

The seas in Michael Finlay's ears washed over lunch with Andy Sweeting, they washed over history, they washed over games in PE, they washed him up the road off the bus, to the brink of the hole in the road. The hole they were filling in.

'You can't do that,' Michael Finlay gaped at the ancient shales. The shales that were fast disappearing under buckets and buckets of rubble. 'You're not filling the holes in *already*?'

'Job's done,' the water man said. *Avalon Water Services Limited*, said his bright orange nylon jacket. *Our Standards Are Yours.* 'Time to clear up the mess,' he said. 'I expect you'll be glad when it's over.'

'My mum will, I won't,' Michael Finlay said. The hiss of ancient seas washed every thought away. He wanted to add, Thanks for showing me what's under the road. Thanks for making me see things completely differently, for showing me the sea-bed, a thousand feet of mud in layers like pages you could read, if you wanted, like a book. Thanks for showing me seas I could swim in if I stood here and the times of the world were different, and continents slid and volcanoes boiled and we slid down under the sea, down in the great Devonian, when fishes gaped you'd never believe, and all we were was a lump on a bigger lump, somewhere under the equator . . . Instead, he said, 'Thanks for fixing the water.'

'No problem.' The water man waved.

Michael Finlay stood and watched that hole filled in, and he didn't say a word or move a muscle when at last the Devonian slates saw the sky for the very last time in what would very probably be his, Mickey Finn's lifetime, then vanished under backfill and tarmac. What could he do, but remember them?

In the end he did nothing but go up the road to the sewage works. The water men were packing away. A line of forlorn-looking bowsers put their tap-ends together and shared a quiet yarn with one another. They would be hauled on, now, to the next place that needed its pipes rehabilitating, and the next place after that. As Michael watched, a man in an orange jacket took down the sign that said, CAUTION – SITE ENTRANCE and packed it away in a van. They would take down other signs saying, DIVERTED TRAFFIC and ROAD CLOSED. Even the exciting MULTIPLE EXCAVATIONS AHEAD would have to go. They would come back later for their pumps and rigs and skips and boxes of metal pipe junctions, their manhole covers and flying red tape, their traffic cones and their fencing.

After the water men had gone, the seas in Michael Finlay's head settled and seemed to subside. Sure, he felt sea-sick now and again. Sometimes the ground seemed queasy under his feet. If he looked out of his bedroom window with his eyes half closed long enough, he could *feel* that the house was afloat on a tide of time. There was nothing solid that would *always* be there when you wanted it, nothing at all. He tried to put water out of his mind. But everything he heard or saw, for some pointed reason, made him think of it.

More rain this month, the weather forecaster boomed out of the telly, than in *any other February* since records began. February Fill-Dyke, his grandfather called it. When would it ever stop raining? The film trailer only made it worse. On breakfast TV, it featured an asteroid hitting the earth. It could happen, the trailer said. Less than five hours' warning. Are *you* ready for the Flood?

Other things had happened. Nothing easily explained. Nothing you'd notice on its own, but they all added up to something . . . *watery*. In the library, for instance, water leaked in on Michael's neck. It had never happened before. The librarian didn't know why, but water was coming in. She put a bucket under the drip, and it dripped all the time Michael read. Just before he left the library, he crossed in front of the fiction shelves, and a book jumped out in front of him. *Things To Come*, the book was called. Michael put it back. But that night he dreamed a dream that raised the hair on his head.

He dreamed he walked in the country lanes near his home, but from every side the lanes filled up with water, so he couldn't get back home again, no matter *how* he tried. Familiar roads became rivers, and the more he swam and struggled and jumped from hedge to hedge, the more the rivers swept him away, and the torrent seemed never-ending – and when he went to look for his brother, his brother had no eyes.

He refused to go swimming next day. The light-filled pool in school looked a tad too much like a warm, deep sea to Michael Finlay. All that water – how could he know what would happen? He even stopped washing his hair. The feel of the water on his head filled him with a feeling of dread.

'What's the matter with you, you're not *washing*,' Stuart said.

'Plenty of time for that,' Michael said, mysteriously, and swam off to look up deep-sea fishes in his bedroom.

'Pooh!' Stuart said, as he passed. 'Someone niffs around here.'

'Probably you,' Michael told him.

'*I* don't pretend I'm swimming and never go in the pool.'

'So shout about it, why don't you?'

'I will, if you want,' Stuart said. 'I really think someone should know.'

Michael avoided the next swimming lesson at school. He forged a note saying, 'Michael's stitches must be kept dry.' He didn't say where the stitches were. He swam around the house late at night, and the seas grew loud in his ears.

Next evening, his mother ran a bath. 'You're getting in,' she said. 'Now.'

But Michael Finlay didn't get in. Instead he wet his face and hair and splashed around a bit. He wasn't about to immerse himself in *water*. What was their hurry? The water would rise all too soon. Back in the Devonian the water had risen, Michael knew, more than five feet in a person's lifetime – say, seventy years – that was *two hundred feet world-wide*. The world with its cities and people were

105

specks in geological time. Continents shifted. Seas came and went. Would it – could it ever – was it *bound* to happen again?

'What if an asteroid hit us?' he asked his mother.

His mother considered. 'What if it didn't?'

'It could cause a flood, though, couldn't it?'

'I suppose it could, if it happened.'

Michael went to bed that night more thoughtfully than ever. The rain lashed the roof outside. It drummed on his bedroom window. He booted up the computer. He looked up ASTEROIDS. If an asteroid three miles across hit Bermuda, a wave a hundred feet high would hit New York. There would be fire storms in London. *Thirty per cent of the UK would be under water in no time*. Michael Finlay jumped up and parted his curtains. He looked out on dark Cap Hill and its sea-bed valley, far below. *Which thirty per cent would be under water?* he wondered. *Would the lapping waves of a new sea reach all the way up to Cap Hill?*

The day after that was a Saturday. 'Coming up Cap Hill after lunch?' Michael asked Stuart mid-morning.

'Why?' Stuart asked.

'Why not?' *To save you, of course, don't you know?* Michael Finlay cleared his throat. 'We could take the football round the rings. Play a bit, go up the café.'

'OK.' Stuart considered. 'I've got nothing better to do.'

They knocked a ball about for quite a while on Cap Hill. Cap Hill looked down on the valley, the river, the city – the sea, on the far horizon. It was chilly and wild, with the wind tearing through their hair and battering Cap Hill Pike, the pile of granite pancakes on the top. It was always cold on Cap Hill. The wind blew ceaselessly, day and night, never stopping for anything. It had stripped away the soil from the top of the hill and left the Pike exposed like a pile of badly balanced plates. Under the plates, or pancakes, the rings of an Iron Age fort made a good place to mess about. Michael and Stuart Finlay kicked a ball around the rings under the Pike – they made the ball bounce unpredictably – and the wind shrilled through their jumpers and the world unrolled beneath them away to the far horizon, where the city made busy shapes and the clouds collected over them, as they'd collected over the sea in aeons before, before cities had ever been thought of. Even the rings of the Iron Age fort had been built, Michael thought, only yesterday in geological time. You could practically see the For Sale sign, the Iron Age rings were so new. Attractive circular development. Good views. For sale by arrangement with people in skins with axes . . .

'I'm tired,' Stuart said. 'Let's stop now.'

Michael Finlay stopped. He flung himself down with his brother on the topmost Iron Age ring and considered the world spread beneath them, sparkling out towards the horizon where the sea made a line of light.

'What's that name for a tidal wave?' Michael asked his brother.

'A *tsunami*,' Stuart said, who'd been doing tidal waves at school.

Michael saw the *tsunami* in his mind. It would roll in from the far horizon over the village below and the village hall where the Talk was, over the buried holes in the road and the departed men who had buried them, over the pub, the garage, the shops, the school, the newsagent, over the caravan park, the quays on the river and the river itself, the church, the cemetery, and the playgroup. Over the city, with its cinemas, bus station, department stores, railways, pavilions, DIY stores, bowling alleys, YMCA, Smith's, Woollie's, Boots. Over parks and flowers and gardens. Over everything.

It would cover everything. It was lapping their feet even now. That new tide would darken the horizon and it would rush up Cap Hill before anyone realised what was happening and leave nothing at all behind it, except perhaps only the very top – the stones, perhaps, would stick up – the *very top of the hill*. Yes, Michael thought, it would leave Cap Hill Pike. Cap Hill Pike would stick up like a thumb in the flood to mark what was lost and what *had* been. He would be safe if he could climb the Pike and stand on its very top, safe and alone in a drowned world – a drowned world you couldn't tell from a drowned world a long time before, where sullen, half-formed fishes roved and the three-hundred-and-ninety-five-*million*-year-old Devonian sky hung fire over smouldering volcanoes. If someone –

'What's up?' Stuart asked.

'I'm thinking, all right? Do you mind?'

– if someone slipped him a Mickey Finn and he slept for millions of years – like that man in the story who slept a long time, what was his name? Rip Van Winkle? – if someone slipped him a Mickey Finn and he did an *extra-long Rip Van Winkle*, he would see that sea fill, he knew. Another several million years, and the sea might be gone yet again. Another village might spring up. Another village Talk. Another Michael Finlay, to sit on a hill and think it out. Round and round and round. Like the water. Like everything else. The river and its valley unrolled beneath him to the horizon. It had been a sea *and it would be again*, he could *see* it. That dream about lanes filling up and eyes disappearing. Maybe they'd all be blind fishes again, who knew?

Michael Finlay got up and began to climb Cap Hill Pike.

To start with, Stuart watched him. 'Hey, Michael, what are you doing?'

Pretty soon, Stuart got up. 'What are you doing?' he said. 'Hey, you can't climb that.'

'I want to see how high it is.' Michael hauled himself from stone to stone, and the granite barked his hands and knees. 'I just want to see if I can.'

'You shouldn't do that,' Stuart said. 'Mikey, it's too high.'

Michael Finlay pulled himself up onto the next stone, and the next. Lucky for him they'd been weathered into great, flat, rough-faced shanks like the sides of whales. They weren't too hard to climb – if you didn't look down. The overhangs were the worst, as the edge of each stone pancake grew steeper and wider. Higher and higher he climbed, way *too* high, he knew.

'Mikey, that's enough! Stop and come down now, all right?'

Michael Finlay looked down. Stuart's head looked pea-sized. He'd better not fall off. He'd better give the Pike his full attention. Two more stones to go, big rough stones, with no obvious holds, that took off your skin if you brushed them. The granite felt like shark-skin or something – it was hard to shake off the feeling that he was climbing a very big fish. Every time he reached for a hold, the shark-skin barked his elbows. Every time he hauled up a notch, he breathed in the smell of the stones – a smell like moss and moor-water, like earth and wind and volcanoes, moulding this tower, these stones, this place, just so he, Michael Finlay, could climb it.

Mikey . . . Was that Stuart? *Mikey* . . . *please come down* . . .

His knees were bleeding. His legs had turned to jelly. The strength had gone from his arms. His nose was running, his eyes were streaming, his

111

muscles screaming. One more overhang to go.
Handhold. Toehold. Lean and reach. Handhold.
Toehold. Lean and reach. Michael Finlay was
practically sobbing when he hauled himself up,
triumphantly, on the topmost pancake of Cap Hill
Pike, in the teeth of the gale that had shaped it.

Mikey . . . please . . . don't . . .

The topmost stone was a teeterer, barely
balanced at all. It was stand or fall. No turning
back. Michael Finlay straightened warily, and the
wind slammed into his face and thrummed in his
clothes and tore back his hair and inflated the
sides of his nostrils so he could hardly breathe. He
threw out his arms and took it all in – the wind,
the hill, the view – the sparkling sea in a silver-
bright line, so much clearer now, on the horizon.

Mikey . . . what can you see . . . ?

'*THE SEA!*' he shouted. '*I SEE IT!*' But the
wind stopped the words in his throat.

And will it rise up? Mikey, will it?

'WHAT DID YOU SAY, STU – IS THAT
YOU?'

He couldn't tell any more. But the anxious
voice whispered on: *Will it rise up and drown us
all . . . ?*

'MAYBE IT WILL.'

112

Tell me it won't . . . What's the point . . . if everything's going to be drowned?

'MAYBE IT WON'T.'

I keep hearing the sea all the time . . . Mikey, I'm worried, will it . . . ?

'WHY ASK ME?'

You might as well throw yourself off . . . as drown . . .

'HOW DO I KNOW WHAT'LL HAPPEN?'

. . . drowning's not nice, you know . . .

Michael Finlay teetered on the very cusp of Cap Hill Pike. The wind tore spittle from his mouth and battered the clothes on his back. For a moment he let himself wobble. The anxious voice ran on: *Mikey, will the sea come . . . ?*

'I TOLD YOU, I DON'T KNOW.'

. . . what about Mum and Dad . . .

'I THINK AND THINK AND *THINK* AND –'

. . . what about Stu? Stu doesn't swim very well . . .

'I DON'T KNOW ANYTHING AT *ALL*.'

. . . I don't want them all to sink and drown . . . tell me the sea won't come . . . I don't want it to . . .

'HOW CAN I TELL.'

Tears streamed down Michael Finlay's face. He didn't know how to answer the anxious voice in his mind.

'DON'T ASK ME – I DON'T KNOW.'

The silver line of the sea gleamed on the horizon like a promise. And suddenly Michael Finlay *did* know.

'*I CAN SEE THE SEA!*' he bellowed into the wind. '*RIGHT OUT TO DRAGO'S ISLAND!*'

The gun-metal sea lapping Drago's Island made Michael Finlay its promise. It might rise some time in the future. But for now, it would stay in its place.

'YAAAY-AY!' He filled his lungs in the wind. 'HOO-WHOO, GET *THIS*!'

The hill held him up because it was meant to. If the sea had been meant to rush down on him, he'd have gills and fins like a fish. Michael Finlay felt the wind and the sea and the sky holding him safely in his time like a cradle, and he knew he felt solid and real, and the place was a place of danger.

'I'M COMING DOWN!' he shouted. 'I'M COMING DOWN *RIGHT NOW*!'

Michael Finlay sat down. Through streaming tears whipped up, and away, by the wind, he finally cleared his mind of ancient seas. The sea would rise, but not in *his* lifetime. Not in so many lifetimes to come. One day it would rise. Gingerly he lay on his stomach and felt the granite rasp his face. Bit by bit, little by little, he allowed his legs to dangle. At last his feet made contact with the giant stone below. With enormous concentration, step by fearful step, tearing his knees and elbows as he went, Michael Finlay descended Cap Hill Pike to meet his brother's fury at the bottom.

'YOU PRAT!' Stuart exploded, 'I mean *big-time*! What did you do *that* for? Didn't you hear me *calling* you? Didn't you hear me shouting COME DOWN NOW?'

'Sorry,' Michael said, 'I couldn't hear a thing.'

'Supposing you fell off the top? I thought you were going to fall off the top. Supposing you fell off the top and I had to go home?'

'Well, I didn't,' Michael said, 'so no one has to know.'

'You're a madman, you know that? Don't *ever* do that to me again.'

'Sorry. I didn't mean to.'

'Fine. That's all right, then.'

'Feels brilliant up there. You can see the sea really well.'

'Can you see Home Park?' Stuart named the city football ground.

'You can see Home Park *and* the lights over the pitch, plus the bridge and the Eddystone Lighthouse.'

'Nice one,' Stuart said.

'Shame it'll all be gone one day.'

'What d'you mean?' Stuart said, 'when will it all be gone?'

'A long time in the future, you know? Hundreds of millions of years? Everything changes,' Michael said. 'Nothing's here for ever.'

'I know that,' Stuart said.

'Millions of years ago, right, this all used to be under the sea.'

'You told me,' Stuart said.

'And one day it will be again – all covered in water. But not in our lifetimes, of course.'

'Cool,' Stuart said. 'Shall we go down the café?'

That night Michael Finlay ran a bath. He lay back luxuriously and soaked his poor knees and elbows and – *ow!* – the water really stung. He squeezed it through his sponge and thought about Things To Come. They would come whatever he did. He didn't even worry about the melting

Larsen B glacier in the Antarctic, when an Action-peace circular came around. He would do what he could not to contribute to global warming. He hoped the glacier wouldn't melt, but maybe it was going to melt anyway. He probably should worry, but what could he do to halt geological time or the turn and turnabout of the ages? He showered every day like he used to. He opened his bedroom curtains. He left off swimming around the house and took up swimming at school.

In time, he quite forgot how funny he'd been about water. But he never forgot the Talk in the village hall. He never forgot the hiss of Devonian seas. And even after it was filled in and quite forgotten, Michael Finlay felt the hole in the road at the bus stop through the bottoms of his shoes and up through his very *bones* when he stood over it every day and waited for the bus which would take him to school. Those ancient shales had marked him — probably the reason he became a Marine Engineer and gave a talk on Ancient Undersea Cliffs and Coastlines of the Cap River Estuary Grounds in, as they say, the fullness of time — and in the undersea world of Michael Finlay, time was *always* full.

CAR SICK

Ever been really car-sick? Pale as paper? Hating the *smell* of cars? With parents that just don't *get* it, like mine?

My olds don't *understand* about car-sickness. They don't know what it's like to be just-about-all right until the car tilts a certain way or the heater's up too much or the plastic smell of the seats just tips you over the edge. They sit merrily upfront arguing or whatever else they do, and they don't understand at all. Have *they* ever felt like hurling every time the car takes a bridge or a hairpin, a bump or even a *traffic light*?

Excuse me if I feel quite strongly about this, but I *do* suffer most weekends. Most weekends I spend hours in the car with my parents with my stomach swilling around like a milk factory, and then there's the embarrassment, when Dad gets road rage on wheels. 'Let's go out,' he says. 'Let's go for a run in the country.' He drives, like, *all afternoon* through villages called Piddle Henbottom or Little Stuffit, then finally he stops at a pub with no family room and it's Coke and crisps in the car for yours truly, thank *you* very much. Cars. I tell you, I'm *sick* of 'em

The Tantra's not a bad car. *Your Tantra represents an ideal synthesis of advanced technology, outstanding safety, environmental compatibility and economy in operation*, the Owner's Manual says. I have plenty of time to read the Owner's Manual when I'm stuck in the car outside a pub. The Tantra offers technical sophistication and exceptional comfort. It's just that I'm sick of it. We go out motoring — that's what the olds call it, motoring — we go out motoring most weekends, mainly to garden centres and stately homes, steam rallies, fêtes, you name it. My olds're a lot older than most people's. I don't think they meant to have me. I think I was quite a surprise.

The joys of motoring, they say. Apart from the odd cream tea and a bag of crisps at a pub, I'd like to know what they *are*. I said to 'em, 'Let *me* drive. You sit there, heartless parents. See what it feels like, endlessly going somewhere you don't know, feeling sick, with no idea when feeling sick will *ever end*, when you never wanted to come out *anyway.* Oh, and throw in dying of embarrassment and fear every time your driver — that's me — throws a wobbly in a car park or on a one-way system in some fume-filled, gridlocked town centre.'

I'm kidding, of course. I never said, 'Let me drive.' But I've felt like it plenty of times. Especially the day we had one of Dad's little runs in the country — I thought we'd *never* get there — about eighty miles plus wrong turnings and wild-goose chases (we do a lot of those) to Bullimore Wildlife Park. So we're going along, and Dad says to Mum, 'Where's the map?'

'Map?' Mum says. 'What map?'

'Are we nearly there?' I say. 'I'm feeling really sick.'

'The map,' Dad says, 'of West Dorset.'

'South and East Wiltshire,' Mum says, 'Hampshire, Somerset.' She surfaces from the car pocket with Devon and South East Cornwall. 'No West Dorset here, I'm afraid.'

'I'm sick,' I say. 'Can't we stop?'

'I thought you'd got Robert some pills,' Dad says.

'I did,' Mum says. 'Robert, have you taken those pills?'

'Yes,' I lie. 'I took two.'

'Well, then, you'll be just fine.'

'Right,' I say, 'you'd know.'

Let me tell you about travel-sickness pills. Travel-sickness pills are like torches and glue – they don't work. My mate Christow went up to London on the coach not so long ago. He goes, 'I got my travel sickness pills. I took two before I got on.' Know what he goes and does? My mate Steve Christow only goes and downs a whole bag of Flumps and takes a seat over the heaters. Then he's surprised he chucks up half-way. So much for travel-sickness pills. They came up whole, Christow says. They hadn't even dissolved.

So I don't take pills, I put up with it. Some people say you grow out of travel-sickness. 'Don't worry,' they say, 'you'll grow out of it.' The way you grow out of curly hair or sticking-out ears, I suppose. Some people say it's all in your mind. The power of suggestion, etc. I'd like to suggest to *them* they sit in the back of our car on a winding country road, in summer, with the windows done up because Dad won't have them down. The car vents, you see, are an adequate draught for anyone. Except someone with their guts in their mouth.

I'm sorry, but that's how it feels. Especially when Dad never stops.

Usually we go on and on, because Dad can't decide where to pull in, or he doesn't *want* to pull in until he finds the ultimate pit-stop, so he goes on and on and *on*, past pubs offering grub, family rooms, warmth, puppies, discos, their fortune, bank account and villa in *Spain* if you'll only pull in, except that Dad won't, until even *Mum* feels faint and begs him to stop.

Sometimes a toilet break works. 'I need a toilet,' I say. 'I have to have one *now*.' It's usually good for a five-minute stop in a field or a breath of fresh air at some petrol station where Dad stocks up on wine gums and soft drinks so he can keep going on for *ever*. They can't ignore the toilet call, the way they can car-sickness – I've only ever actually chucked up once in the car, and that was when I was three, so naturally it's all in my mind and I'm making it up – so toilet stops are one way to make Dad pull in when I get really desperate. Except once it backfired badly.

The only reason I'm even *mentioning* the Exit Seventeen Episode, is to show you how bad it gets. We're on the motorway, right, when I want to go, like, *badly*. Dad says, 'Hang on, Robert.

Services twenty miles.' Then what happens? He only 'forgets' and misses the Branscombe Services exit – exit sixteen, that is – my last chance for forty-seven miles. Well, I don't think I need to spell it out. I think you can see what's coming. After I'd filled up our sandwich box behind the car off exit seventeen with half of southern England speeding past, I felt like I'd hit rock bottom. Whatever the filling in the Terminal Sandwich of Motorway Shame was, I'd eaten it with mayo. And all because Dad couldn't stop.

So we're going along to Bullimore, and: 'Are you all right, Robert?' Mum goes.

'No,' I say, 'I'm dying.'

'Won't be long now. Almost there.'

They always say that. It's supposed to make you feel better.

'You can't go wrong if you look straight ahead.' Dad checks me in his mirror. 'Eyes on the horizon, that's the way.'

'Pull yourself together. Eyes on the horizon.' They always say that, as well. Let me deal with this one. Keeping your eyes on the horizon when you feel like *visiting* the horizon with half your stomach contents is about as much help as stoking a fire just before it burns the house down. Plus *you* try seeing past Dad's head when he's just got his jaws around half a pound of wine gums. The horizon isn't even in sight.

The day we visit Bullimore I sit in the front half-way, which is all right except for Dad's driving. I decide I'd rather be car-sick than tongue-lashed by Dad for map-reading a nano-second too slowly – reading the map turns my stomach over, anyway – or suggesting we go by any way other than the Official Dad-approved Route. I actually ask him to stop so I can crawl back to my accustomed place of torture, the back seat. You can get used to anything after a while.

So we motor *for ever* and we finally get to Bullimore Wildlife Park about eleven forty-five in the morning, by which time I'm feeling so grisly I just don't *care* any more. I'm thinking they can wrap me up in a car rug and just about go on for *ever* – Chile, Uruguay, Java, what do *I* care? – when Dad knocks a hole in the car park. This is after we drive in at the wrong entrance and a ranger with a mobile phone makes us drive out again, which makes Dad mad to start with. Then what happens is, he reverses and doesn't see the post. Of course, right away it's the post's fault.

'What the *devil* – ?'

'Clive,' Mum says, 'we've hit a post.'

'I can see that,' Dad says. 'I'm not stupid. What the hell is it *doing* there?'

He jams the car into first gear and shoots forward, then into reverse and goes back, then forward again, then back, swearing a lot in between. Pretty soon, people are staring. After two hours in the car I already feel like the last crisp in the packet. Now I feel like crying, but I don't.

At last Dad stops the car. Christow and me get out. I didn't mention before we had Christow with us. My parents never understand why I want a mate along. 'It's nice,' they say, 'just the three of us. Why do you want Steven Christow?' Why do they *think* I want someone my own age along? I can't exactly say, So I can have some *fun*. To break the tension, you know? Mum, Dad, me, me, Mum, Dad. Just the three of us. It's so intense sometimes. They wouldn't understand if I told them. My parents are just so *old*, you know? They don't understand a thing.

So after we hit the post in the car park at Bullimore Wildlife Park, Christow helps me out of the car. After chucking up Flumps on the London Rapide, he understands how I'm feeling. I don't actually dry-heave in the bushes, but for a while I come close. After my mouth stops watering I just feel sort of light-headed, like I'm here but it's not really me. That's how I normally feel when we arrive anywhere in the car. Usually I'm just beginning to feel all right again when I have to get back in to go back home. But not this time. This time we have to examine the car in detail, once Dad finally has it parked. I have plenty of time to sit down and get over motion-sickness. Motion-sickness has nothing on embarrassment once Dad gets out of his pram. He gets out and kicks the post. 'Ruddy thing,' he says. 'They want their bumps felt,' he says. 'Putting ruddy posts in, just under the line of people's vision.'

For once, I'm feeling OK. The Tantra's OK, too, once Dad can actually see it through the red mist of rage over his eyes. Damage is minimal, considering. Only a bash on the bumper. A knocked-over wooden post. And most people thinking we're mad.

'Could be worse,' Christow jokes. 'Could've been concrete or something.'

'That's right,' Dad says. 'We're lucky to get into the car park so lightly. We ought to be grateful they haven't mined it or put up rolls of barbed wire.'

'Now, Clive,' Mum says, 'take the chairs out.'

'We shan't want the chairs until later.'

'I'm only meaning,' Mum says, 'take out the chairs from under the picnic. Did I not tell you that flask's got to be right side up?'

'Not in the last five minutes, you didn't,' Dad says. 'I don't think I heard Mum say Right Side Up in the last five minutes, did you, Steven?'

Christow doesn't understand Dad's sense of humour. *I* don't understand Dad's sense of humour. Plus he actually calls Mum, *Mum*, as in: 'Have you packed the salt and pepper, Mum?' or: 'Ask Mum if she's heard.' It isn't so bad when it's just the three of us – I've kind of got used to it, you know? But with friends around Dad's a nightmare, he really is. It's actually so bad I had to try to ask him not to do it. 'I've got Christow coming,' I said. 'Can you not call Mum Mum?'

'What?' Dad said. 'I like that. I'll call Mum anything I like.'

So just because I ask him not to, he calls Mum Mum even more. He really overdoes it in the Grazing Animals and Elephants Compound. Mum's never been so be-Mummed.

'Would that be a baby giraffe, Mum, what do you think?'

'Looks like it, doesn't it?' Mum says.

'Antelope in far west of compound, it says here. Elephants to your right. Approach All Animals with Caution. Drive-Through Predator and Monkey Park – we'll probably do that after lunch. Then there's Hippo Lake. What about it, Mum? Shall we do that after lunch?'

'What are you asking *me* for?' Mum says. 'Would you boys like to go off on your own, and we'll all meet up again later?'

Later is one o'clock for warmish egg-and-salad-cream sandwiches and even warmer lemonade – I hate lemonade, what makes anyone *like* it? – after Christow and I at least get to see the elephants without Dad asking Mum what she thinks of them. Christow and I think they're smart. Especially the baby elephants. They rush up to the fence as soon as they see us and feel us all over with their trunks. I never realised baby elephants have wiry black bristles sticking out all over their backs, but they do. You should go to Bullimore and feel 'em.

Dad makes Christow sit on an aluminium fold-out chair and balance a plastic plate on his knee to eat his lunch. I really want a picture of that. 'Dad, can I take a picture?' I jump up and hold out my hand.

He hands me the camera after he's given me a million instructions for taking a snap with it, the way he always has to. I don't take it straight away. First I leave my Swiss roll.

'Not eating much, Robert?' Dad says.

'I can't really, can I?' I say. 'Not if you don't want me being sick all over the back of the car on the way home.'

'Get something down you,' Dad barks. 'No wonder you look like a ghost.'

I back off so I get Bullimore House in the background, then – snap! I take the picture at the moment Dad's adjusting his trousers. Always good for a laugh.

I hate him, I tell the camera. *If I could make him sick, I would*.

'Go on, Dad, have mine,' I say, when I get back onto the car rug. 'I don't really like warm Swiss roll. You might as well finish it up.'

'Don't mind if I do,' Dad says, polishing off a Scotch egg.

'Have some more tea, as well.' Christow watches me tip in sugar. 'How about Hippo Lake after?'

'After what?' Dad asks, troughing down Swiss roll and sweet tea.

'After lunch, you said. Want my last sandwich, as well?'

Christow reads out the leaflet. ' "Hippo Lake and Crocodile Alley. Waterproof Coats for Hire. Not for the faint-hearted," it says here. Can we do that next?'

'I think I might go for a walk,' Dad says. 'Which way did it say to the toilets?'

Dad wanders off to find the toilets. When he comes back he's actually been to the shop and brought himself a cold beer as well. His face shines. The sun beats down. 'It's hot,' he says. 'Chin, chin.'

After lunch we finally get out on to Hippo Lake after the olds try their best to get out of it. They try to make out they'd rather walk the Flamingo Trail and come back round by the rhinos. At least, that's what Dad makes out.

'Come on, Dad,' I say. 'The boat looks really good. Plus you can take some pictures.'

'I don't know,' Dad says doubtfully. 'I think Mum wants a walk – you want a walk, don't you, Mum?'

'I don't know what I want, really.' Mum's giving the White Water Ride the eye. 'It looks quite exciting,' she says.

We join the queue anyway, arguing. Hippo

Lake looks cool. Basically, there's this huge great lake with an island and boats go around it on a tour and hippos pop up – if you're lucky – and you take a picture of them, or you can buy a picture of them afterwards that looks like a snap you *might've* taken of them if they *don't* pop up, which they might not. Or you can buy a Combined Ticket for Crocodile Alley, and go down the White Water rapids as well, which is favourite with Christow and me.

'There's buffalo compounds two and three on the Flamingo Trail, it says here.' Dad whips out his brochure again. 'We could come back round by the rhinos.'

'I can't believe you still want to go on a *walk*.'

'I haven't lost the use of my legs yet, Robert.'

'Don't you fancy the boats, or what?'

'Not madly, no, I don't.'

'Come on, Dad, what's the difference?' He's not getting out of it that easily. ' "White Water Thrills," it says here. You might as well go in a boat as walk around in this heat.'

I'm looking after Dad's interests. I'm cunning when I want to be, see?

'Robert's right,' Mum says. 'It's too hot to walk in this heat.'

'I don't really feel,' Dad says, 'like being trussed up in a plastic mac.'

'You can always get wet, if you want.' Christow's enjoying this, now.

'What's that?'

'Get some white water down you,' I say. 'No wonder you run into posts.'

'I'm not sure,' Dad says, looking vaguely like thunder, 'I'm not sure I *need* Hippo Lake.'

'Oh, come on, Clive,' Mum says, 'you really are an old woman.'

'Well, thanks very much,' Dad says. 'I don't *think*,' Dad says, 'I've done anything to deserve *that*.'

We reach the edge of the quay and use our Combined Tickets. Mum and Dad hire see-through plastic macs that do up under their chins and make them look like pre-packed instant dinners, and we climb into this daggy old tourist showboat with about twenty other people also done up in plastic, all except Christow and me and a few other kids who'd rather be wet than sad. Dad doesn't look too happy, but he's in.

So we get out on to Hippo Lake, and the first thing that happens is, we find out the wind's got up and it isn't as calm as it looks. The deck rolls a bit but Dad gets his feet under the seat in front of him and pulls out his camera and soon he's snapping away at completely blank stretches of water where hippos' ears might have been sighted at some distant time in the past. We circle Baboon Island with no baboons in sight. Then we get out the bait buckets and chuck bloody bits of fish over the side, but still no joy with the hippos, which are veggies anyway, as even Christow points out, but this doesn't stop all the olds on board snapping away with their cameras like maniacs, when suddenly *seals* pop up all around us, and they really are the business – I mean, they're great. They're really close, so you can see their big sad eyes and their whiskers and their funny, closed-in ears and the mottled marks on their skins. Christow and me bung them *loads* of fish. And then we're back at the jetty and into Crocodile Alley.

We change boats for Crocodile Alley. At this point, Dad looks upset. The sun's pretty fierce by now. Dad's plastic mac has completely steamed up. He looks like a jar of pickled eggs.

'What's the matter, Clive?' Mum says.

'Feel a bit squiffy, actually.' Dad burps into his hand. 'I shouldn't have eaten cucumber. Cucumber never agrees with me.'

'It doesn't agree with beer and eggs,' Mum reminds him. 'I thought you were eating a lot,' Mum says, 'but I didn't say at the time.'

So we're all four of us sat in this bright blue inflatable, when it slides off down Crocodile Alley, Christow and me really up for it, Dad up for something else, probably.

'You think they'd give you a dry boat at least,' Dad complains. 'These seats are soaking wet and there's quite a lot of water in the –'

The first wave hits us in the face just as we're going round a bend. Christow and I hang on and shout like madmen. The next bend flings us straight down this funnel into a whirlpool, then along this canal with tanks of real crocs either side. They can't get at us, of course, but they're so close you can see they'd like to. We bang against both sides of the canal and spin round lots of times, then we get sucked down some rapids that throw Mum and Dad together, then throw them apart again. Dad isn't enjoying himself. He hangs on and looks really green.

'NOT LONG NOW!' I shout to Dad.

'WHAT?' Dad looks like death. 'I CAN'T HEAR A THING YOU'RE –'

'BRILLIANT, ISN'T IT?'

Dad doesn't think it's brilliant. He looks like he'll throw up his guts. Before I have a chance to feel sorry for him, a wave smashes me right in the face. *NOT FEELING SICK, ARE WE? HANG ON TIGHT AND SUFFER, YOU SELFISH, UNFEELING OLD BLIMP.* That's not what I shout, but I feel like it. He can't hear a thing in the rapids. I *could* shout anything I like.

'COME ON, DAD! STOP MAKING A FUSS ABOUT NOTHING!'

We go *down* a chute and *round* some kind of island and *over* a weir into a splash-pool, which rolls us round a bend and into some kind of tunnel – and *out* of the tunnel into daylight, and serious white water. Poor old Dad. He grips the side. I almost feel sorry for him this time.

'DOESN'T FEEL TOO GOOD, DOES IT?'

'Uh?'

'EYES ON THE HORIZON! PULL YOURSELF TOGETHER! COME ON – YOU'RE ALL RIGHT!'

'ROBERT! WHAT ARE YOU SHOUT-ING ABOUT?' Mum puts her hand over mine. She's doing well. Her eyes are bright. She's had the ride of her life. 'IS IT NEARLY OVER NOW?' she shouts.

It *is* nearly over. So's Dad – nearly over the side. As we swirl into calmer waters and the high-pressure jets hit us, making sure we finish wet through if we're not completely soaked already, poor Dad's blowing chunks over the side of the boat, and the back of his neck's really red. No one looks back to see the trail we've made in the water, but I guess it features ham and eggs, Swiss roll and cucumber. Christow and I look at each other. Chucking up Flumps on the London Rapide has nothing on polluting the entire White Water Ride system at Bullimore Wildlife Park in front of a million people, thank *you* very much. Whatever the filling in the Terminal Sandwich of Theme Park Shame, Dad just ate it with flags on.

No one does anything much for quite a long time after that. Christow and me do stickers in the *Wildlife Wonders* book Mum scores in the shop, a bit childish really, but I like childish things sometimes. Mum packs up the boot. Dad lies down and groans. After he's had a good lie-down on the rug in the shade of the Tantra and Mum's finished packing away the picnic, we all climb back into the car.

No one says anything.

Then: 'What's next?' says Christow. 'That was brilliant.'

Mum says, 'What was brilliant?'

'Hippo Lake.'

Dad groans.

'Plus Crocodile Alley was *cool*.'

The back of his neck's faintly green. Dad starts up the car.

'Not going yet, are we?' I ask. 'What about the *Drive-Thru Predator & Monkey Park*?' I ask. 'Aren't we going to drive through them?'

Dad puts the car into gear. 'I can do without monkeys,' he says.

The drive home's a big improvement on the drive out, I have to say. For one thing, Dad doesn't argue. He leaves Mum to navigate, and Mum gets on and navigates us to a pub where there's this cool family room with bar-billiards and video games and the sausage and chips is really good. Dad drinks mineral water quietly and doesn't say very much, but Christow and I play Defenders and Grand Prix and Spacehogs and I wipe Christow *out* at bar-billiards, but he takes it well because he's Christow.

Dad takes the motorway almost all the rest of the way home, and it's fast and straight, so I don't feel sick hardly at all. He doesn't bother with villages named Whiddle Piddlington or Up Barfing or twisty roads or churches or anything. I can't tell him how much better it is, so I don't even try. I'm suddenly glad I didn't laugh at him, when he was throwing up off the boat. I felt like it, but I didn't. Because I know how it feels.

'Why can't we always go on the motorway?' I ask.

'It's not very picturesque,' Mum says.

'No,' I say, 'but it's straighter.'

'Good, wasn't it?' Christow says. 'The elephants, I mean. And the seals. I liked the seals, did you like the seals Mrs Rendell?'

'I liked Crocodile Alley,' Mum says. 'I thought it was really astounding.'

'Feeling all right, Robert?' Dad asks.

'Brilliant, thanks,' I say. 'Thanks for going a straight way home. It makes a lot of difference.'

'Pity about the monkeys,' Christow says.

'You don't want to bother with monkeys,' Dad says. 'Those monkeys,' Dad says, 'all they do is snap off your radio aerial and peel off your window trim. Bloke at work drove his Vectra through that monkey park and the monkeys pulled off his wipers. He left his window trim in the road. *And* his tow-bar cover.'

Dad checks me out in his rear-view mirror. I smile, and Dad smiles back. He still looks pale — he still doesn't know how I'm feeling. Is it his fault he's old and he knows it? But somehow I have a feeling Dad just might be more sympathetic in future. He might choose straight roads more often. He might even open some windows. If I'm car-sick, he'll understand.

'Dad's right,' I say. 'Who *cares* about seeing monkeys? I'm *sick* of monkeys,' I say.

BIGGLESMITH!!

'Shel, *don't*, I mean it.'

Shel and Nina Gibbons lay helplessly on the floor. Or Nina Gibbons did, anyway. Her sister Michelle was getting on top of her this time. Literally. Every time she play-fought Shel, Shel had the upper hand. Strong as a wire monkey, Shel was tough and agile and *nothing* could throw her off.

'I'm not in the mood, Shel, don't –'

Usually Shel would sit on Nina and pin down her arms with her knees and do disgusting things like gob on her face or blow raspberries or roar in her ears. Then there was tickling, and bird's nest. Bird's nest reduced Nina Gibbons to helplessness even just *thinking* about it. Her limbs turned to water. Her strength leaked away in pleading laughter. She became completely helpless and unable to resist Shel at all. And did Shel ever know it.

'No! Not bird's nest! Please!'

Shel produced a finger in mid-air. 'Here's a birdie wants a nest —'

'Don't, Shel, I *mean* it!'

'— a nest in a nice, warm place —'

Nina felt her limbs turn to water. 'Don't,' she begged, 'Shel, don't.'

'— and it's coming in to find it —' Shel wiggled her finger and brought it inexorably closer '— and any minute now, it'll —'

'Stop — I don't want it — *no!*'

Nina made a huge effort to throw her sister off. But Michelle was bigger and stronger. Her sister's wiggling finger zeroed inexorably in.

'— here it comes —'

'SHEL, GET OFF ME!'

'— here comes the birdie to nest in your —'

Nina twisted hysterically.

'— NECK!'

The finger wiggled, paused — then darted in and 'nested' under Nina's chin, where she absolutely couldn't *bear* it, in the most ticklish niche of her neck.

'Shel, don't, please don't, please, Shel —'

Nina Gibbons wasn't in the mood for fighting today, she really wasn't. Sometimes fighting was fun. More often it started out fun and then got an edge of annoyance. The trouble was, as usual, the mood was on a knife edge. The feeling of not being able to stop the tickling, whatever she did, made her helpless before the tickling started. Also it made her annoyed. Why couldn't Shel see? Now and again, she didn't mind. But when she *did* mind – like today she minded – why couldn't Shel understand?

'Stop it, Shel, I'm not joking!' Nina fought her sister off, weakly, desperately, knowing she couldn't win. 'Get *off* me, will you? I'm not in the mood!'

No matter how much she begged or struggled or ordered her off, Shel would always sit on her *just that bit* too long. That was Shel's trouble. She didn't know when to stop. Nina twisted and wriggled, getting really angry, this time. 'Get off me, Shel. *I really mean it this time!*'

'Ah,' Shel said, 'she means it.' And tickled her sister some more.

Nina Gibbons shrieked, 'Get off, I'll wet myself!'

'You better not.'

'I *will*.'

'Shame she can't get up.'

Bigglesmith!

'Get off me, *right now, Michelle Gibbons*!'

Nina Gibbons went mad. Erupting from all directions at once, she bit and kicked and heaved and struggled, this time in deadly earnest. The struggle got vicious, stalemated for a moment or two with both sisters straining for a hold over each other's legs, then Nina lost it completely, flailing her arms and legs like she meant to shake them off.

'Can't you tell when I've had enough – I mean it, *get off me now*!'

Two or three really vicious bangs on the back, and Michelle Gibbons got off her sister at last. And not a moment too soon. 'Hey,' she said, in an injured tone, 'hey, that really hurt.'

'I told you MILLIONS of times to get off,' Nina flamed, in capital letters, really upset this time. 'You always go on too long. NEVER do that to me again.'

'No need to hit me like *that*.'

'When I say get off I MEAN IT. I *hate* the way you don't stop.'

'So half-bang my *back* in, why don't you? How was I to know?'

'You never listen, whatever I say. Can't you *hear* I mean it?'

'Not really. I thought you were laughing.'

'Oh, yeah. I *sound* like I'm laughing.'

Shel shrugged. 'I thought you liked us mucking about.'

'I would, if you knew when to stop.'

'Oh, and you do?'

'I do, as it happens, which is more than *you'll* ever know.'

'Calm down.'

'I *am* calm, thank you.'

Nina Gibbons wiped her face with her sleeve. Her rage had spent itself. But she'd felt like half *killing* her sister. Where was the sense in *that*?

'OK,' she began. 'We're going to *fix* this once and for all.'

'Oh, yeah?' Michelle examined her back in the bedroom mirror. 'See those red marks where you bashed me?'

'Yes, well, I didn't mean to. What we need to do,' Nina Gibbons said carefully, 'what we need to do, is think of a *word*.'

'What word?'

'A word you only use when you really *mean* it. A word you can say to stop fighting — or whatever — and when you *use* that word, that's *it*.'

Michelle pulled down her sweater again.

'Mmm,' she said, 'that's not bad.'

'This word, you don't use it too often, right? But when you do, the other person has to stop *right away*, no matter what they're doing. And this word means you're *desperate*, so no more bird's nest.'

'OK,' Michelle said, 'I get it. So what's the word?'

'The word is . . .' Nina Gibbons thought furiously. Something memorable, something funny, something you could screech out with the full weight of fury behind it, something odd, something final, something . . . 'The word is –'

'Malaga!'

'What?'

'Malaga!'

'I heard you. Why?'

'I don't know.' Shel shrugged. 'Denise Sumner's going to Malaga on holiday this year.'

'Oh,' Nina said, 'good reason.'

'How about Brad, or Paul Nicholls?'

'What – you're actually going to stop tickling me if I yell Brad or Paul?'

'I might.' Shel considered. 'Then again I might not.'

'It has to be something – big. Something we don't forget.'

'Champagne Supernova?' Shel suggested.

'Supercalifragilisticexpi –'

'No, I don't think so.'

'Plinth?'

'Warthog?'

'The indices on the hypotenuse?'

'Snappy one, that.'

'British summertime?'

'Jellyfish?'

'Intestines?'

'*Intestines?*'

'Irritable Bowel Syndrome?'

'Excuse me?'

'Callisthenics?'

'I'm not lying on the floor yelling Callis-thenics! What *are* callisthenics?'

'I don't know,' Nina admitted. 'How about custard pudding?'

'Crusty Semolina!'

'Big Fat Eskimo Toenails!'

'Rubbery Wellies!'

'Bigglesmith!'

'*What?*'

'You heard me, *BIGGLESMITH!*' Nina yelled it this time.

'Bigglesmith.' Meaty, beaty, big and bouncy, it

was a word you wouldn't forget in a hurry. It was a big word with a big – and quite silly – ring to it. A ring you couldn't ignore. Shel rolled the word round her mouth. A slow smile spread to her eyes and made her face quite pleasant.

'Bigglesmith. That's *it*.'

'Bones of Contention,' introduced Freeman Leland, 'will be a Complementary Studies extension featuring *debate*. Anything from capital punishment to genetic engineering. Your lesson, your time, *your* debate.'

'What about hunt protestors?' Colin Denton demanded.

'What about them?'

'Do we hang them or clone them?'

'Colin, that's for you to debate, and for me to regret you want to.'

Freeman Leland smiled. The faint American twang in his voice made him sound cool and reasonable, no matter what he said.

'It isn't funny, Colin. How would *you* like to be hunted?' Nina Gibbons put in.

'Um, I think I'd like it.' Denton grinned, and his face sank into his neck and his neck sank into his chest and the rest of him quivered in the smug, self-satisfied way that made Nina Gibbons want to hit him.

Nina felt her flesh crawl. As well as having a dimpled bum-chin and being physically repulsive, Denton shot small animals with air rifles at weekends. She knew, without having to think about it, that whatever side she was on in any school debate, Colin Denton would be on the other. No matter what it was about. 'You're just weird,' she said.

'I'm calling this series of debates *Bones* for now,' went on Freeman Leland, 'and I hope we can worry some interesting bones of contention between us and really hone our debating skills in this Complementary Studies extension. It's going to be whatever you make of it. And if you think of a better title you'd better let me know.'

That'd be right, Nina thought. Freeman Leland Rules – If That's OK With You. Easily the coolest teacher in school, Freeman Leland liked to think he had a way of putting things which made students feel they'd *contributed*. That was his whole approach. It didn't always work, especially with insects like Denton. But that didn't put him out. Freeman Leland was keen on student input. Keen on debate of all kinds. Keen on *talking things through*.

Nina and Shel had spent serious time imagining him over breakfast. *Can you pass the butter, if you feel you can make that commitment? Would I like some porridge? That's for me to decide and for you to let me. Toast? It's a value judgement — can I get back to you on that one?*

'We can talk about anything, right?' David Rainer asked.

'Anything voted interesting enough to discuss.'

'So we *can't* talk about anything.'

'It's up to you to put it across. *You* sell it to *us* for discussion.'

'What's the point?'

'The point?'

David Rainer frowned. David Rainer was dark and intense and no one messed him about. 'Nothing's going to change things. What's the point in talking?'

'Things like?'

'I don't know. Stuff we do in geography. Over-population in Pradha province. Creeping deforestation. What's the point in *debating* it? Nothing's going to fix it.'

'There's no debate, if we all agree,' Freeman Leland agreed. 'We're not going to save the world. What we want is a bone of contention.'

'Something no one agrees with?'

'Something it's possible to *dis*agree with. You throw us a bone, we'll gnaw it,' Freeman Leland invited. 'Anyone else here think talking about things is pointless?'

'It is if you have ANTS,' Nina Gibbons bowled him.

'ANTS?'

'Automatic Negative Thoughts.'

'Right,' David said sarcastically, 'lots of people have those.'

''Specially hunt protestors.' Colin Denton rippled, his chin disappearing into his neck fat.

'I'm delighted you're getting behind this, Ten GB,' Freeman Leland congratulated the class. 'Plenty of input from everyone makes for a lively discussion. If you'd like a topic discussed, would you run it by me before Friday? You don't have to, of course. You can simply propose it in class. It's your debate, after all.'

'How about journalism?' Nina Gibbons said. 'Journalists get a lot of stick, but *I* think they do a good job. Plus they stand in battle zones —'

'This is Nina Gibbons for *News at Ten*.' Denton put on a newscaster's voice. 'Reports are coming in that I'm changing my name, because most of my fan mail's from monkeys –'

'Something else stupid from Denton.' Nina made a face. 'Why doesn't that surprise me?'

David Rainer thought ethics in journalism might make a pretty good topic, but no one ever knew why because Richard Fargo fell off his chair and brought Martin Rickard down with him. Noise levels rose pretty quickly after that. Freeman Leland raised his voice: 'In the event that no one tables a motion –'

'I tabled Rickard, sir,' Richard Fargo volunteered. 'We're playing bar-billiards, right, and I tripped him up with my cue and decked him on the table –'

'In-the-event-that-no-one-tables-a-motion –'

'Sir, what kind of motion?' Richard Fargo widened his eyes. Someone made a straining noise. 'Would that be a *regular* motion?'

By the time he'd explained that *tabling a motion* meant proposing a topic for discussion in a certain formalised way so that everyone else could disagree with it, Freeman Leland had completely lost control of the class. Nina watched him scornfully. Freeman Leland was weak. He meant well, but his big puffy words were weak. Words widdled out of his mouth. They didn't mean anything at all.

'Could I have your attention, Ten GB? If no one tables a topic for next week's Bones – Richard Fargo and Martin Rickard, I assume you're getting up to present a topic for discussion?'

'I was, but now I'm not.' Richard Fargo sat down again. Martin Rickard sat down on top of him.

'One student per chair please, Martin.'

Freeman Leland waited until Martin Rickard had seated himself noisily behind Richard Fargo. Then he cleared his throat. 'Unless anyone has a serious contribution, next week's Bones will take the form of an open debate on what we'd all like to talk about. Thank you for your attention. And that winds it up for today – except –'

'Except what, Mr Leland?' Denton asked. 'Except I don't have to do it?'

'– except, of course, for the *issues*. Things that concern you and me, things that concern just about everyone. Think about those issues and how you might get them across. Words,' finished Freeman Leland, 'meanings. Thoughts. Conclusions. Between now and next week, okay, let's *think* about what we say.'

Let's *think* about what we say. Nina Gibbons shouldered her bag and walked home with David

Rainer through the Grange Road Mall. The Grange Road Mall was her shortest way home, but it didn't always appeal. Today it appealed less than usual. The warm air, filled with shop smells and faintly tinged with fast food, made her feel slightly ill. She hurried on, feeling different today, somehow special, and found herself reading the signs.

Ginger's for Hair – New Look Styles a Speciality.

Flowers Express – Same Day Blooms Say So Much.

NAILED for Nail Extensions & Facial Makeover.

TANNERS – Medically Approved Sunbed Treatment for Safe & Easy Tanning.

KingBurger Easy-Over Breakfast Only Two Ninety-Nine!

The trouble was, no good shops. The Grange Road Mall had been going downhill for years. It had been glossy once. Once it had been the place to go. Now only sad people shopped there. But, still, they shopped a lot.

Crimpers for Hair and Beauty.

Top Look!

NEW SEASON SALE!

Shoe-be-dos, TRAINERS HALF PRICE.

SuperFare at Grange Rd Mall – Individual Provençal Pies £1.75 All This Week.

The signs were bad. The signs, Nina thought, of the way she'd been brought up to live. How would it look to an Eskimo? Someone from an Eastern bloc country where most of the shelves stood empty? A baby from Pradha province? There was so much on offer. Too much. Why hadn't she noticed the smell of *too much* before? She always walked home through the Grange Road Mall. She didn't always stop. But today she stopped. Today she stopped and lingered . . .

'Come on,' David said, 'what's the matter?'

. . . and it seemed to Nina Gibbons that she was seeing the Grange Road Mall for the very first time in her life. The cheesy-looking glass lift – like Charlie's Great Glass Elevator – whispered up and down between the artificial palms. Above it, the balcony clattered with afternoon shoppers having a quick and crowded cuppa in the Buttery. Everywhere, people shopped.

'Nothing's the matter,' she said. 'I was thinking about Bones of Contention.'

The Sock Shop and the Shirt Shack and the Loose Box racing-themed Snack Spot. Shopping – *wanting things* – never stopped. Like tickling, it ran on and on.

'What are you doing for next week's Bones?'
David asked.

'Something Colin Denton *isn't*. I *hate* Colin
Denton,' Nina told him.

'This is Nina Gibbons for *News at Ten*. Here on
the battlefront, exchanges have been brisk —'

'BIGGLESMITH!' Michelle screamed.

'— with Nina Gibbons coming under con-
tinuous fire and little in the way of —'

'*BIGGLESMITH!*' Michelle screamed again.

'— relief, the light at the end of the tunnel
seems a —'

Nina Gibbons sat on top of her sister and
wound up her outside broadcast.

'— long way away. Get *up*, then,' Nina told
Shel, getting up herself. 'What are you waiting for,
Christmas?'

Where had she got her strength from tonight?
It must be anger with Denton. Or maybe with
her parents, rowing again as usual. It was one of
those evenings for fighting. Anger was in the air.
You could practically *see* it, Nina thought.

'I *said* Bigglesmith.' Michelle got up crossly. 'I
thought you were meant to *respect* it. What's the
point, if you don't?'

'I got up, didn't I?'

'Not right away, you didn't.'

'I'm sorry, *what* did you say?' Nina flicked Shel with a towel.

'*Bigglesmith!*' Shel put the bed between herself and the towel. 'Pack it in, it hurts!'

'Abuse of Bigglesmith, in any case,' Nina accused her. 'You're devaluing Bigglesmith by its overuse in inappropriate contexts.'

'Excuse me?'

'The thing about Bigglesmith is, it's an unbreakable swear-on-your-honour –'

'Can you stop flicking me *now*?'

Nina stopped and sat down. It was getting on her nerves. The row downstairs had been going on since tea-time. Something to do with money – it usually was. Soon Mum and Dad would calm down. It would all blow over, as usual. Why did it have to start?

'Are you all right? Nina?'

'What do *you* think? I *like* hearing them rowing downstairs?'

'It'll be all right. They don't mean it.'

'Why do they *do* it, then?'

'What's the matter with *you*?' Shel said. 'You're really aggro tonight.'

Bigglesmith!

'It's Denton,' Nina lied. It *was* partly Denton, though. 'I really, really hate him. Plus, we're doing debates at school.'

'And?'

'Denton made a prat of himself again today. No one can debate *anything* with Denton around. He doesn't know *how* to debate.'

'So?'

'So I'm trying to think of a topic. But I *know* he'll shout me down.'

'Don't let him.'

'How do I stop him?'

'What's the debate about?'

'Anything. Whatever. We've got to think of things.'

A door slammed somewhere downstairs. Angry voices rose and fell. It was worse, Nina thought, when they stopped.

'They're getting worse,' Shel said.

'The sound of firing seems unceasing, here in these battle-scarred hills –'

'Nina. It isn't funny.'

'No,' Nina said, 'it isn't.' Parents' rows were never funny. 'I never said it was.'

'Hear that crash? They're throwing things.'

'Correction. One of them is.'

'Think Mum's all right?'

'Mum's all right,' Nina said. 'Sounds a lot worse than it is.'

'Should we go down?'

'Too scary.'

'You better be right,' Shel said.

A door opened. A door closed. Then the front door slammed.

'Dad going out, I expect,' Shel said.

'About time.' Nina got up. Her stomach felt filled with angry words. Words she felt like shouting. 'I'm going out – want to come?'

Shel considered. 'What – now?'

'I have to get out, OK?'

Shel shrugged on a jacket. 'OK. All right. I'll come.'

The Grange Road Mall showed its dark side by night, the dank and evil-smelling passages where sad people slumped and slept and sometimes didn't get up. Its everyday face had been blinkered by steel blinds and shutters and PREMISES PROTECTED BY ALLSTAR SECURITY SYSTEMS signs. Apart from American Fry and V. J. Video, a pub or two on the corner and the London Late-Nite Shopper, everything was closed. The tellies in Gleason's

Electrics' window showed highlights of the day's events on *Newsnight Extra*, ten newscasters smiling blandly from ten TV sets with ten different prices – but there wasn't a lot else to see.

Nina pressed her forehead to the window of Gleason's Electrics and allowed herself to feel angry. The news moved on to Bosnia, then Albania. All that arguing, Nina thought. At home and away – wars and disputations, everywhere, all over the place, all the time. If only they stopped to *listen* and *think*. If only they could all *hear*. The Day in Parliament flickered up on all ten tellies at once. 'Order!' the Speaker bleated. 'Order! Gentlemen, please! Order! Order! Order!' But still no order prevailed.

'Got enough for some chips?' Shel asked. 'I've got eighty-three p.'

They rounded the corner on the chip shop. Opposite the chippie, outside a pub called the Three Jacks, something was going on. Something pretty scary. Something involving David Rainer.

'What is it?' Nina stared. 'Looks like *David Rainer*.'

Three figures – three Jacks, maybe – had David Rainer on the floor. Nina could hear the blows land. It wasn't a friendly bundle. They were really kicking him in.

'Nina, come back!' Shel screamed. 'Nina! Come – back – here!'

Through the legs of the psychos kicking him in, Nina glimpsed his face across the dirty, fag-littered floor. David Rainer's eyes appealed to Nina Gibbons across the length of the Grange Road Mall. She had time to notice *the exact pattern* of the floor tiles before she started running.

'*STOP!*' she shouted, running. '*DON'T YOU DARE! YOU JUST LEAVE HIM ALONE!*'

David Rainer lay curled on the ground. For long and horrible moments, whenever they wanted, wherever they could, the three jacks stood and kicked him. Then the moment ended. The three jacks looked up.

'GET OFF HIM!' Nina Gibbons shouted. 'DON'T YOU KNOW WHEN TO STOP? *GET OFF HIM AND LEAVE HIM ALONE!*'

Time seemed to pass really slowly. '*Nina, come back!*' Michelle screamed. David Rainer looked curled-up and small. The back of his neck looked red. Nina Gibbons shouted and shouted and shouted, without thinking, without knowing, without stopping. She didn't know what she shouted. She'd never made so much noise.

'BIGGLESMITH!' she shouted.

Whaat?

'BIGGLESMITH! BIGGLESMITH! BIG-GLESMITH!'

The three jacks were running away.

Shut that noisy cow up! Leave it! Come on! Now!

Nina watched them go, screaming she didn't know what, so long as it was LOUD and David Rainer's eyes were closed and they didn't look at her that way any more, the way they'd looked at her a moment ago, across the chip-littered, dirty floor. She shouted through fear and anger. Then she shouted through blood. She hadn't known she'd bitten her cheek until she'd opened her mouth and yelled.

And in the Grange Road Mall, with its fountains, she'd shouted, '*BIGGLESMITH!*'

'Got a topic, have we?' Denton asked, unpleasantly.

'That's for me to know and for you to find out.'

Nina made her Denton face, a particularly acid smile. It usually shut him up. She checked her notes for *Bones*. She'd tabled the motion. Run it by Freeman Leland. What else could she do, but look a lot better than she felt? Starting a killer debate, with her arguments thought out before-hand, was the least she could do for Denton. And even that was kind. *Don't let him shout you down*, Shel had said. *Say what you think and stick to it.*

'Wait for it, Denton,' she told him.

Freeman Leland cleared his throat. 'So far in Bones of Contention, I'm pleased to say we've covered a lot of ground. Topics so far have included bloodsports,' he looked at Colin Denton, 'home-lessness, the death penalty, should zoos be abolished and, last week, violence on television. The motion before the house this week has been tabled by Nina Gibbons —'

'And seconded by monkeys.' Denton grinned.

'You'll have your chance in a moment, Colin.' Freeman Leland frowned. 'The motion before this House today is that "Shop till you drop is an immoral idea. When is enough enough, in view of Third World want?" Have we a seconder?'

Everyone looked at Nina. Nina felt waves of panic. She might have put it better. She saw now, they wouldn't understand. But someone under-stood. David Rainer held her with his hunted-looking eyes.

'I'll second that, sir,' he said. 'I can't put up my hand.'

Bigglesmith!

'Winded by running in from maths, Mr Rainer?' Freeman Leland joked.

David Rainer winced. He wore Elastoplast from brow to cheekbone. It made him almost good-looking. 'Something like that, sir,' he said.

'. . . and as a confirmed shopper, I'd just like to say *enough shopping*.' Nina Gibbons wound up her argument for ethical shopping. She felt she'd put it well. Better, at least, than the motion she'd tabled earlier. 'When we're kids our mums and dads tell us when enough is enough. Now we can buy almost anything we want, we have to learn to say it for ourselves.'

'Why?' asked Colin Denton.

'Ethical shopping means only buying things you *need*, made by people who get paid a decent rate. Else we're robbing someone, somewhere.'

'Why?' asked Colin Denton.

'Don't you ever feel there's too much choice?' Nina floundered a little under the Denton stare. 'Like, you go into the supermarket and there's just *too much* of everything and it's obscene that we need it all?'

'No,' said Colin Denton.

'Me neither,' said Richard Fargo.

'And there's stuff like mange-tout peas and

people in Zambia are paid, like, one *p* to pick them, and the supermarkets charge a *pound*.'

'So,' Denton said, 'what's that to you?'

'Like you never go shopping or something,' Martin Rickard put in.

'I *do*, that's the point.'

'You think you're so big with your *ethics*,' Denton sneered.

'No,' Nina said, 'I don't.'

'Why don't you take your monge-the-toot whatsits and –'

'I just think we could all have less, not more, and no one would even mind.'

'– why don't you go and –'

'Enough. That's all I'm saying.'

'– get *stuffed*.'

'Arooo! Ar-ar-arooo!' Richard Fargo threw back his head and howled like a wolf for no other reason than that he felt like it. 'Ar-ar-aroo!'

Nina felt tears welling up. Couldn't *anyone* see what she meant?

'Let's get back to basics,' Freeman Leland reasoned. 'Is it or isn't it reasonable in a consumer society, to want to –'

'She loves herself,' Denton said.

'Shut it,' said David Rainer.

Bigglesmith!

'She loves herself to death –'

'Nina fancies gibbons,' Richard Fargo added.

'– and they love *her* –'

'Shut *up!*' David shouted.

'– that's why she's got hairy arms –'

'– arms? did you see her *legs*?'

'I told you, shut it *now!*'

'Nina Gibbons –'

'Tells some big ones –'

'*Leave her alone, why don't you?*'

'She's got fleas –'

'On her knees –'

'BIGGLESMITH!' David shouted. '*Don't you know when to stop?*'

'So,' said Freeman Leland, over a hot chocolate, 'what does it *mean*, exactly? Enough's enough? Stop doing whatever it is you're doing? Sit up and *listen* to me, will you?'

'All of those things.' Nina nodded. 'Plus, it means this is *it*.'

'It, what?'

'It – *I mean what I'm saying.* Like in the Second World War, when Hitler invaded Poland, we should've said Bigglesmith!'

Denton, Rainer, Rickard and Fargo nodded

sagely and agreed. Fargo had bolted his milk-shake already. Already busy angling for another, he wasn't too busy to nick Martin Rickard's chips. He would eat what he could while it lasted. It wasn't *every* day Complementary Studies went to town. Not every day they finished a debate with Coke 'n' chips at Kingburger, courtesy of Freeman Leland. But this would be the last time. The motion is carried, Freeman Leland had said. This House believes that *enough is enough*. This brings our series of debates to an end. Shall we celebrate?

That would be the end of debates, Fargo wasn't sure why. What had it all been about? Nina Gibbons had got pretty mad. Rainer went ape at Denton. Then he'd shouted that word. That word had changed things, somehow. What did that word *mean*?

'It's a big word,' Leland said. 'It takes a lot of courage.'

'There's other big words,' Nina said.

'Bigglesmith's special,' said Denton.

'Look inside,' David said. 'That's what Biggle-smith means.'

'And listen up,' Denton added. 'It means listen up, as well.'

'It saved me last night,' David said.

Bigglesmith!

'Where was it, again?' Fargo asked.

'Over there, under the sign.' David pointed through the window at the Three Jacks pub sign opposite. 'Right outside the Three Jacks. That's where it saved me,' he said.

Everyone considered the spot reverently. David had told them all about it. How three kids had kicked him in when he'd gone out to get some milk at the Late-Nite Shopper. How he'd thought he was in for it, until Nina Gibbons showed up. How she'd run towards him – when she could have run away – and shouted and shouted and *shouted*:'BIGGLESMITH GET OFF HIM! BIGGLESMITH STOP NOW! BIGGLE-SMITH! BIGGLESMITH! BIGGLESMITH!' How it had freaked out the kids who jumped him when they didn't understand what it meant. How they'd nicked off without a thing. How *Bigglesmith!* had saved him. How it kind of came out when he needed it. How he couldn't forget it, ever, now he'd got it inside his head.

'What were they like?' Denton asked.

'Three kids. I don't know.' David Rainer shrugged. 'They didn't get anything.'

'Good for Bigglesmith.' Freeman Leland smiled. 'It's quite a concept, Nina.'

'I know it's silly, really.' Nina grinned. '*I* don't know what it means.'

But everyone else did, it seemed. *Bigglesmith!* had reached them all. Even Colin Denton.

'I think it just means stop what you're doing and *think*,' Martin Rickard put in.

'That as well,' Denton said.

Freeman Leland nodded. 'It seems to mean *integrity* also.'

'I know what's right,' David Rainer offered, 'and I'll stick by what I say.'

'Exactly,' agreed Freeman Leland. 'Character. Trust. Honesty. Meaning what you say.'

'Right,' Denton nodded, 'that's the one. It means all that, as well.'

'It kind of means *enough*, too,' Nina added thoughtfully. Everything she'd tried to say seemed to boil down to this word. 'Enough-and-be-thankful, kind of.'

'*Bigglesmith!* means all of it,' David Rainer agreed.

'It's a kind of feeling there's no words for.' Richard Fargo surprised himself. 'That's what *I* think, anyway.'

'Plus it means time to *think*,' Martin Rickard insisted.

Bigglesmith!

Integrity. Honesty. Stop and Enough. It meant something different to everyone. *Bigglesmith!* had grown big and meaningful, Nina thought, with the power everyone had given it who *wanted* a truthful word which made what people thought *count*. More power to its elbow, if it could. In a world full of words no one listened to, there was nothing a spear of justice like *Bigglesmith!* couldn't do. Think of the things it *might've* done. Old Anne Boleyn might've yelled it and kept her head. Elizabeth the First might've yelled it and stopped the Armada. If their daughters popped up and yelled it, it might even stop parents rowing. At least, it might make them laugh.

Bigglesmith! would *make* people listen. And once they'd stopped and listened, they would have to stop and think. How about **Bigglesmith!** on the world's nuclear waste transporters? It could become a watchword. A quiet word. A people's word. It was a people's word already. It belonged to everyone who could say it and *feel* what it meant.

'The world needs a word like Bigglesmith!' Freeman Leland said, thoughtfully.

'That's just what I was thinking,' Nina Gibbons nodded. 'And, you know? I think –'

'Yes?'

'I think maybe, just maybe, if I get to be a journalist, I might be going to tell them.'

'That's just what they want,' David said. 'Outspoken people like you.'

'It's what they're going to *get*.'

'You have a *dooty*.' David smiled. 'Get out there and spread the Word.'

'She's started already,' Denton said.

'In the beginning, was the Word. And the Word was —'

'*Bigglesmith!*'

Nina smiled. 'You got it.'

STUFF POLICE

The day he borrowed his brother Aran's bike and carelessly left it propped against the dustbins overnight was a very special day for Justin Needham. He didn't know it at the time. But next morning, he pretty soon knew it. Next morning Justin Needham looked out of his bedroom window and felt ever so slightly sick. The reason was the dustmen. And what the dustmen had done. Or what the dustmen had *taken*, to be precise.

Oh, no! The bin-men had been! Aran's bike — where was it???

They'd taken his brother Aran's mountain bike. The mountain bike he, Justin Needham, had had special dispensation to borrow for *only one evening*. He'd only left it out the front — against the bins, admittedly. How *could* they have taken it away? What were they, stupid? Couldn't the dust-men *see* it hadn't been put out with the rubbish, even though it looked as if it had? The whole horrendous situation flashed on Justin Needham in an instant. It wasn't a new bike, admittedly. It looked pretty scuzzy and old. The dustmen *did* take big items away. Plus, he'd thrown the bike down by the bins last night as his dad had been putting them out. He'd meant to go back and put it away. He hadn't known *this* would happen.

Slowly the scale of what actually *had* happened percolated through the brain of Justin Needham. Aran wasn't going to like it. Aran was large and peevish. He especially liked his well-used and customised mountain bike. He rode it most weekends. Today was Friday. Friday Trials up Mine Trax was a popular event. Aran would want his mountain bike as soon as he got in from work. 'Chain it round the front when you've finished,' Aran had said, when he, Justin, had begged to borrow his, Aran's, bike the previous night. 'I'm going up Engels' tomorrow. So make sure it's round the front.'

Aran meant Terry Engels. He and Terry Engels and Simon 'Madman' Madeley rode up on the mine most Friday nights and thrashed around in the silt, one reason Aran's bike looked like a tank had driven over it. Now, probably, a tank — or a JCB — *would* drive over Aran's bike. At the dump.

Or the yard. Wherever they took these things. Justin Needham swallowed. This was big. He'd only forgotten to put a *bike* away. The consequences of his *not* having put the stupid bike away were, like, out of all proportion. This was like forgetting to pick up your sandwiches and starting the Third World War. *Chain it round the front when you've finished.* He'd left it round the front, all right. It was just that he'd forgotten to chain it. Forgotten to prop it against the wall. Forgotten all about it. He'd really blown it this time. So he had a rep for leaving things – stuff, mainly – for leaving *stuff* lying around. This was something special. No one would give him a chance to explain. It would be so *typical* of him.

Justin Needham pressed his face to the window and looked up and down the road. The dustbin lids lay where the bin-men had thrown them down in their neck-breaking rush to get through their rounds and off for their elevenses. Hang on a minute. One of the lids was still spinning – the bin men had only just gone!

Justin Needham flung himself down the stairs and into the road outside. 'Hullo?' he shouted, 'excuse me?' he raced to the corner. *'Please wait!'*

But the dustmen were long gone. Long gone,

too, was any last glimpse of Aran's bike. Justin sat down on the pavement. What now? he wondered. Another bike? *By two o'clock in the afternoon, when Aran finished his shift?* Aran hadn't even left for work yet. Justin got up and dusted off his hands. He had to keep it together until Aran had left the house. He'd think about replacement bikes, or whatever, with Aran safely out of the way on the early shift at Kingburger.

So where *did* the dustmen take things? Justin had never actually thought about it before. He tried hard and pictured a rubbish dump at the end of the world under a bloody red sunset. He pictured his brother's bike collapsing under a crusher, its sad remaining components picked over and splatted by gulls. How could this have *happened*? To him, Justin Needham? Maybe he should just tell Aran and get it over with. Justin pictured telling Aran his bike had been taken away. Then he lidded the bins and took them in.

'Nice work, Justin,' his father said. 'And while you're at it you can bring in that stuff in the garden.'

Justin sighed. 'OK.' So he left things lying around sometimes. What was it? Crime of the century?

Then he had an inspiration. 'You didn't bring Aran's bike in last night?'

'No. Why?'

'I just thought you might've brought it in.'

'Why are you asking me?'

'No problem,' Justin lied. 'I just thought you might have moved it.'

'You didn't tidy your room last night?'

'No, but I thought about it.'

He didn't feel like breakfast. But Justin ate some anyway. His father got ready to run Aran to work. After he'd run Aran to work he'd come home and gripe at Justin, unless Justin got out of his way. Justin's dad worked from home. That's what he called it, working from home. But mainly he worked from the armchair in the living room where he sat and watched telly most days.

Aran put his head round the door. 'Hey, Bungle, what did I say?'

'What did you say about what?'

Aran called Justin 'Bungle' sometimes. There wasn't a lot he could do.

'My bike, duffo. Round the front. Didn't you get what I said?'

Justin's nerve-endings tingled. *Hey, pizza-brain, it's down the dump. Try riding it after that.* 'It's round the back,' he lied, coolly. 'I'll get it in a minute.'

'Just so it's there when I get in from work.' Aran put on his Kingburger hat. 'See you later, losers.'

The car coughed out of the driveway and chugged away up the road. Justin waited a moment or two, then wandered up to the lay-by where the bin-men sometimes pulled in for a fag and a Thermos, on the off-chance he'd see or hear them. He walked crisply back with the din of birds in his ears and neither sight nor sound of the dustcart with its straining jaws chewing up the stuff people had fed it, and the dirty old dolls and teddy-bears the dustmen had rescued from the rubbish bobbing sadly along in front.

'What happens, you know, when the dustmen take things away?' Justin asked his father, when he'd got back.

'They take it down the dump.'

'Then what?'

'Some of it gets recycled.' Justin's father shrugged. 'Some of it gets sent away.'

'Where does it get sent away to?'

'The land-fill site, I think. Most of it goes there to start with.'

'What about big things, though? Things like —'

'Washing machines? Bound to get recycled.'

What about bikes? Justin wanted to say. *Especially bikes taken away by mistake*. He pictured Aran's mountain bike getting recycled. Then he said: 'They don't get melted down, or anything?'

'Probably. How would I know?'

Justin digested this. Then he said: 'They might probably take things home?'

'Who?'

'The dustmen? If someone throws something away, and it's still, like, really good? Like a bike or a cooker or something?'

'They might, I suppose, I don't know.' Justin's dad shook out the paper and sat down with it in a don't-bother-me-any-more kind of way. 'Why all this interest in dustmen?'

Justin had another inspiration. 'Where *is* the dump?' he asked.

'Curtain Road, I suppose,' his father said. 'Look it up in the phone book. And pick up that stuff on the stairs while you're at it. It's been there at least three days.'

Justin looked it up. *County Environmental Services*, the phone book said. *Curtain Road Re-*

cycling Centre, Open Six Days a Week. Curtain Road was in Moorstock, some seven or eight miles away. How to get there to find a bike, with no bike to get there *on?*

'Have you picked up that stuff on the stairs yet?' his father asked him.

'Just going out, but I will.'

'How about the stuff in the garden?'

Justin dodged out before his father could get into it. So what if he left stuff lying around on the stairs? What was it, a few socks or schoolbooks? Pick this up, pick that up. A few little things on the floor, and Dad got out of his pram. He was over-compensating, probably. Trying to prove he could run the house and look after two boys as *well* as being unemployed. He hadn't been the same since he lost his job. His father should get out more. Move *this* stuff, move *that* stuff – what was he, the *stuff police?*

Justin Needham took the eleven-ten bus to Moorstock and sallied out onto Curtain Road at about eleven forty-five. Curtain Road was a long road, which wound its way past Justin's school – closed now, for the holidays – before licking off out to Magwell Crags and the river-meanders beyond *that.* Justin checked the closed-up doors and windows, the silent school halls and playing fields, with enormous satisfaction. Easter holidays. Way to go. Two and a half weeks of glorious freedom, and no one to tell you how to use it or make you feel bad you hadn't handed in something complicated they'd dreamed up for you to do, just so they could sit on it for three months before handing it back for you to mark yourself, in the interests of Self Assessment. It was so stupid. How do you feel you've coped with this project? Brilliantly, of course. How many marks do I give myself? A★ plus three million, plus an honours degree and a silver cup – what did you *think* I'd give myself? A raspberry?

Justin slowed. CURTAIN ROAD RE-CYCLING CENTRE, said the sign. OPEN SIX DAYS A WEEK.

So here he was at the dump. So why was he so nervous? Of course they'd realise his brother's bike'd been brought there by mistake, if he explained it. It wouldn't be, like, the only mistake in the *world*. It was easy to explain – wasn't it? *Good morning, you know you handle large items? Well, I'm looking for a black Snakebite Series 2 mountain bike, pretty beat up – oh, right, it came in this morning? Yeah – a mistake, too right – that's brilliant, thanks a lot.*

Another five minutes, and it would've gone in the crusher? My lucky day? No kidding. Probably it would go easily. Probably he'd be out and away in five minutes. Probably things got taken away by mistake all the time. Probably he'd better go in.

Justin wandered in. The roar of a reversing caterpillar-track crane, straining to pull something almost too large for it out of a pile of scrap-metal, took the words right out of his mouth as he tried, at least three times, to explain what he was looking for to the strange-looking man in the tin shed by the entrance. The strange-looking man in the tin shed by the entrance just narrowed his eyes and nodded, whatever Justin said, and pointed down to the dump. Justin was pretty sure he hadn't heard a thing. He had an impressive collection of broken clocks in his shed. Justin wondered what he did with them. Probably he tried to get them going.

A dumb row of broken washing machines lined the lane down to the main dump and the land-fill beyond. Justin's spirits rose. He couldn't help but notice one or two bikes in amongst the rolls of old carpet and noxious old settees. This was the Large Items dump. It held everything from hot-water tanks to wardrobes, dishwashers, fridges, tumble-driers, rotting beds and mattresses, push-chairs and broken office equipment, anything, in fact, too large to sink in the land-fill, with some reclaimable parts. So far, so good. All he had to do now was find out where the dustcarts came in. And what had come in that morning. Twelve o'clock. The dustcart must have come in by *now*. Probably it was out on the land-fill, where all the gulls were wheeling. But would it have checked into Large Items first to off-load Aran's bike? The man in the tin shed must know.

Justin almost turned back to ask him. But it was no use. He'd never make Tin Shed under-stand. Tin Shed's mind had been blunted by staying too long at the dump. No wonder, when the dump was a nightmare. Never, Justin thought, never had he seen so much *stuff*. No wonder Tin Shed had gone a bit strange with so much *stuff* building up round his shed, so that his shed grew darker and darker and might even disappear some day under the odds and ends and Large Items of *other people's lives* . . .

'Looking for something?'

'I'm sorry?' Justin spun round. A tall man. In grey. Behind him. Where had *he* sprung from? he wondered.

'I said, are you looking for something?' the stranger repeated.

Justin Needham stared. 'Um. I don't think — not really.'

The man in the grey coat nodded. 'Anything you want here. You only have to look.'

'I didn't know dumps were like this,' Justin said.

The man in the grey coat looked at him. 'What did you think they were like?'

Justin walked back down the lane. He would ask Tin Shed where the dustcarts came in. Then he would find Aran's bike. Then he would get off home, and be in before two o'clock.

'I live in the house down the road,' the stranger said, falling in beside Justin. 'Want to come back and see it?'

'Not really,' Justin said edgily. 'I just want my brother's bike.'

The stranger stopped. 'Is it a Snakebite Series 2? Handlebars a bit twisted?'

'That's the one.' Justin's heart almost stopped. 'Did you — have you seen it?'

'Fifteen gears?'

'Right.'

'Alloy rims? Water bottle and cage?'

'Check.'

'Carbon steel frame, the worse for wear?'

'Whatever – have you seen it?'

'Seen it?' The stranger smiled. 'I rescued it this morning.'

'You rescued it this morning?' Glorious, golden words. Justin had to repeat them.

'I thought it might be a mistake. It's only round the corner. Back with the rest of my stuff.'

'It was an accident, see?' Relief flooded Justin's voice. This man had Aran's bike. He was going to get it back. His chest eased at last. He became quite confidential. 'My brother, see, he lent me his bike, because – well, you don't want to know –'

'Yes, I do,' the stranger said. 'Why don't we get it while you tell me?'

'– and my dad, he's always saying, why don't you pick up your stuff? So next time, I probably will. Put away Aran's bike, I mean, else he'll kill me. But it's funny how things just pile up, and the next thing you know there's just *millions* –'

'Tell me about it,' Lomax said. 'See all the stuff around *here*?'

Justin drank his tea and looked around. The man in grey wasn't a stranger any more, after all.

He was the man with Aran's bike at his house, name of Lomax. That was how Justin Needham squared going home with a stranger. Lomax watched him squaring it. Once they were in at his garden gate, he gave Justin time to settle. He let him look around the yard. He even invited him in.

'Come in,' Lomax said, 'why don't you?'

'I can't,' Justin said. 'I shouldn't.'

'The name's Lomax,' Lomax said. 'And you are?'

'Just going,' said Justin.

'I'll get your brother's bike,' Lomax said, 'if you give me half a tick. Come in a bit and sit down,' he said, 'it's not as if you don't know me. Not now we've been introduced.'

Justin sneezed. 'It's dusty.'

'It's this stuff,' Lomax said. 'It owns me. I can't even *give* it away.'

Lomax wasn't kidding. His house and yard and garden groaned with *stuff* brought home from the dump – dusty, useless, dog-eared stuff, stuff no one would willingly lumber themselves with if they could bring themselves to throw it away. Bikes and baths; carpets and car-parts; chicken-coops and chairs; pig-arks and prams; pews and mangles and barrows and blocks and dressers and tellies and half a fairground ride – or, at least, the cars off the ride. Plus a washing-line hung entirely with old leather gloves, and a stack of timber and roof tiles that ran all the way down to the car-hulks along by the wall. The wall itself was hung with mole-traps. Beyond that stood an old chaise-longue settee, and beyond *that* a whole half-a-boat.

Inside Lomax's house, the stuff had settled. There had been plenty of time – bags and bags of time – for *stuff* to settle into every corner under a thick layer of dust. Pots and pans and stags' heads; brollies and skeletons and tailor's dummies; stuffed quails and carriage-clocks; fire-irons and ice-picks; butterflies and butter-pats; comics and motor-bike parts; lava-lamps and leaping salmon in not-so-leaping glass cases; monkey-wrenches and socket-sets; boxes of cogs and badges, screws and grommets and washers; sink-plungers and sump oil; bottles and boots and bags and shoes and hats and *windowsills* full of frosted mineral quartzes and sea-shells fuzzed with dust – all the *stuff* of the world had settled in nicely at Lomax's house and got its feet under the table. It had made itself quite at home. Unlike Justin Needham.

Justin was staying a *minute*, that was all. Lomax

was weird but OK, plus the door stood open — plus he needed the bike. He hadn't actually *seen* Aran's bike. Lomax would get it in a minute.

'Take a seat while I get the bike,' Lomax had said, opening the door. 'I'm done in, how about you?'

He *looked* done in, Justin thought, with his grey-looking skin and his tired eyes and his fumbling, fiddling fingers. Lomax had shrugged off his coat to put on the kettle. Under his grey coat he wore a grey cardigan over grey-looking trousers. Everything he had on was grey. The house was grey, as well. Justin looked around. Strange growths and lumps grew out of the walls and stairs. It took Justin a moment to realise they were only things covered in dust. Most dust, Justin remembered from something he'd read, most dust was *dead human skin cells*.

'How do you like your tea?'

Justin stared. '*Like* it?'

'Black or white?' Lomax asked. 'With milk or without?'

'With, thanks.' *No dead skin cells, thanks*. 'I shouldn't do this,' Justin said. 'I shouldn't even *be* here.'

'You're right,' Lomax said, making tea. 'It's

never OK to do this. Sugar, or do you want biscuits?'

'This is, like, what my dad would think is horrible.' Justin meant the rubbish-covered garden outside the still-open front door. '*I* don't,' he added quickly, 'but my dad would.'

'It's like what *I* think is horrible. I'm trapped, see?' Lomax swirled the teapot round and round. 'A prisoner of all this stuff. Can't get rid of it. Can't leave it. Completely stuffed, that's me.'

Justin changed the subject. 'Is that the time already?'

A row of fluffy grey clocks on the fluffy grey mantelpiece agreed it was twelve forty-five. He would need a good hour to cycle Aran's bike home before Aran got in and wanted it. He'd need to set out pretty soon.

'My parents said they'd leave me if I didn't clear up my stuff.' Lomax poured the tea. 'That was a long time ago.'

'That's a bit strong,' Justin said.

'I can make it weaker.'

'Your folks, I mean, not the tea.'

'When they said they'd leave me?' Lomax added milk to Justin's tea. The tea was grey like his face. 'Know what happened? They did.'

'They left you? Because you were *untidy*?'

' "Leave me alone," I told them. "Let me live my own life." '

Justin swallowed. 'And did they?'

'What do *you* think?' Lomax laughed sarcastically. 'What do you think all *this* is?'

All *what*? Justin's heart hammered. The lumps on the stairs – what *were* they? They looked like piles of books. A dust-covered guitar. Long-dead plants, a sweater in holes, a frisbee. Records, magazines, schoolbooks. How long had they *been* there? Were these – *Lomax's schoolbooks?*

' "Get off my back," I told them,' Lomax went on. ' "So I don't put stuff away – what are you, the Stuff Police?" '

Justin got up. He felt sick. 'I have to go,' he said. This man had looked inside his mind. *Or the Stuff Police had got him.*

'I told them straight – "So I don't put stuff away for *ten years*, so what?" '

'So you didn't?' Justin said.

'What?'

'Put stuff away for ten years?'

'I *never* put stuff away,' Lomax said. 'See that jigsaw in the corner? I did that in nineteen seventy-four.'

'Excuse me,' Justin said. 'I have to go to the bathroom.'

'Down the hall.' Lomax pointed. 'First door on your left.'

First door on your left. Justin's heart hammered. This strange house. This strange morning. Lomax was freaking him out. Soon – when? – he would go and fetch Aran's bike. Or maybe he wouldn't. *Maybe he never meant to.* Justin gasped for breath. His chest felt like it would burst. He'd leg it out of the bathroom window if he possibly could, tell his dad about the bike, and come back for it later. That was the one. *Out, out, out!* Enough weird things already. Justin followed the dank and smelly corridor, past busts and prints and posters, until the tips of his fingers told him he'd reached the first door on his left.

As soon as the door swung open, he knew there was no way out. The windows in Lomax's bathroom were solid with rust and dirt. The basin and toilet were orange with rust. A fly swam in the pan. There was no escape. There would be nothing for it but to front his way out. Justin wasn't sure he could do it.

Justin Needham re-entered the room briskly.

'OK,' he said brightly. He rubbed his hands. 'Let's go and get that bike.'

'I tried to escape once,' Lomax went on, as though Justin had never gone out. 'Twice, in fact, the last time twelve years ago.'

'See, I've got to ride home straight away,' Justin said, ignoring him. 'Before my brother gets in. It should take me thirty, forty minutes. Forty-five minutes, tops.' Justin checked his watch. 'So can we get the bike, now? If that's OK with you?'

'The first time I tried to escape I was only about your age. Know what I found when I came back?'

'No,' Justin said. 'What?'

'My parents had moved away. They'd left me most of their stuff.'

'What?' Justin said. 'All this?'

'I had to stay and look after it. The stuff wouldn't let me go. I lived alone and nothing changed for years and years and years. But one day, someone came and took my place.' Lomax got up and circled the room. 'The second time I escaped, I stayed away. Merchant seaman for ten years. No room for *stuff* on board ship. I came back two years ago. It's all just the way I left it.' Lomax picked up a book off the stairs. He brushed it off and smiled. 'Outlands Comprehensive, Biology, Miss Smart.' He looked at Justin Needham. 'The stuff on the stairs was covered in dust and right where I left it when I was thirteen, thirty-three years ago.'

Justin stared. 'No kidding.'

'Now I can't get away, you see. I can't just get up and leave it.'

'My mum's just the opposite.' Justin cleared his throat. Lomax wasn't so bad. With parents like that, it wasn't his fault he was weird. 'My mum, she throws things away as soon as they hit ground. She throws stuff away all the time.'

'Ah yes, the Thrower Away.' Lomax put his fingertips together. 'Let me tell you something. There's Hoarders and Ditchers in this world – that's Throwers Away, like your mum.'

'Which am I?' Justin asked.

'You're like me,' Lomax said. 'You're just like I was at your age.'

Thirty-three years ago, Lomax had thrown down his schoolbooks. That made him young in the sixties. Justin looked around. Lava-lamps and posters, magazines and records and a circular plastic chair jumped out in a sixties way. He'd even had a model Dalek from *Doctor Who*. He'd added to it, since them. But the room was like Lomax's time capsule. A capsule that wouldn't let him go.

'Wondering how I got so much *stuff* in the first place?' Lomax asked.

'Not really,' Justin said. '*I must go.*'

'I never tidied my room, see, when I was a kid. I didn't pick stuff up because I didn't think it mattered. My parents did it for me.' Lomax rounded on Justin. 'But let me tell you, boy, stuff has a way of just *lying down on top of you* and clogging up your life. My parents were right, I know now. But I had to learn it the hard way – at the dump.'

'I'm going now,' Justin said.

'I wanted to go, too, but I couldn't,' Lomax said. 'I couldn't get clear of my *stuff*, you see. I'm still not clear of it now.'

'So,' Justin said, 'my brother's bike.'

'So. Your brother's bike.' But Lomax made no move to get it. 'Like a bar of chocolate for the journey?' He rummaged in his pocket. 'These Picnics aren't too bad. I've had 'em since the sixties.'

'Pass,' Justin said. 'Have you tried UFOs? They're lush.'

'UFOs. I've seen 'em.' Lomax unwrapped a Picnic.

'What's your name?' Justin asked, after a moment.

'Name's Lomax. I told you.'

'What's your first name, though?'

'I used to be Justin Lomax. But that was before I had *stuff*. Now I have nothing but trouble, see? Nothing makes me happy.'

Justin? Justin Lomax? The smile fell from Justin's face. He had to pretend he hadn't heard. Weird alarms rang all over. *Now's the time. Get out.* In his confusion, he said, 'Nothing makes you happy? Is that why you took the bike?'

'I didn't take it, I rescued it.'

'So can we get it now?'

Nothing, see? Nothing makes me happy. Everything seemed grey in this house of dust, a house once policed by the Stuff Police, now empty of any feeling except loss and the wish to escape.

'Escape,' breathed the books on the stairs.

'Escape,' whispered the mouldering old palms by the window and the mouldering old hats on the hat-stand, the bags and shoes and bottles, the kinky boots by the door. Escape, escape, escape . . .

'The bike?' Justin insisted.

'Right now?'

'Please.'

'Yes,' said Lomax, 'well, then.'

'Time to go,' Justin said. 'Sorry, it's just that I'm late.'

'It is, indeed, time to go.' Lomax sprang up quite suddenly. 'Follow me, then,' he said. 'You'd better put on this coat.'

'Why do I need a coat?'

'The bike,' Lomax said, 'it's in the cellar.' And he draped his grey coat around Justin. 'You'll need this, too,' Lomax said, and he put his grey hat on Justin's head.

'Just a minute,' Justin said, 'I don't need stuff like this.'

'Oh,' said Lomax, 'I think you do,' and he wheeled out Justin's brother's bike from behind a cupboard door.

'It's not in the cellar at *all*,' Justin said. 'Why didn't you tell me it was there?'

Lomax pushed wide the cluttered front door and the uncluttered sunlight flooded in. One thirty-five, said the line of grey clocks over the grey and ash-choked fireplace. Just twenty-five minutes to cycle home before Aran gets in, Justin thought. He could just about make it if he killed himself. But how could he leave all this stuff?

Lomax cocked a leg over Justin Needham's

brother's bike. 'So long,' he said. 'It's all yours now.'

'What d'you mean — all mine?'

'All this *stuff* — be seeing you.' And Lomax rode out into the sunshine.

'Wait!' Justin cried. 'That's not your bike! Come back!' he cried. *'Mr Lomax!'*

But Lomax peddled off like a madman, down the road, past the dump, down Curtain Road to the school. And as he went he seemed to grow smaller, younger. His back grew narrower, his legs shorter — he seemed bullet-headed, somehow. Like a boy. A boy on a bike.

'Hey, Lomax — Lomax, come back!'

He looked like any other boy would look by the time he drew abreast of the school. Justin Needham rubbed his eyes. His fingers were dirty and grey. He went into the house. He looked in the mirror. 'Mr Lomax?' he said. 'Is that you?'

It wasn't Justin Needham. It wasn't Justin Needham who put on the grimy kettle in the dirty, dust-filled kitchen. Who sat down in the dirty grey chair. Justin Needham had gone.

Gone? It wasn't Justin Needham who looked — again and again — in the mirror. Who clutched his grey face with his hands. Who understood he was trapped, a prisoner of all this *stuff*. He couldn't get rid of it, and he couldn't leave it, *unless someone else took his place* – and who would want to do that?

Justin Lomax brewed his tea and slept in his dirty grey bed, with the stuff of the dump all around him. He could never leave this place. The Stuff Police wouldn't let him. They couldn't make him pick stuff up any more. But they wouldn't let him throw it away. He would never see Aran come home from work. Never come home from school again, and see Dad's pinched-looking face make a smile, where making a smile was an effort. He would bide his time. Some other person who never put stuff away was bound to come along sooner or later. Until then, he could wait.

If he listened *very carefully* he could hear the sound of falling dust. Of slowly gathering skin cells – *his* dead skin cells – slowly falling around him. Lomax picked up a dirty grey record off the stairs. *With the Beatles*, the title read. Lomax looked at the sleeve. Then he opened the lid on an ancient record player. He'd be with the Beatles a long time. He might as well hear them sing.

Nick

It started with *Attack of the Fifty-foot Woman*. That was the film his mother was watching when Charlie Williams first spotted the Spirit of Nicotine. Nick, he called him, for short, when he'd seen him once or twice around the house. Nick rode around on his – Charlie Williams' – mother's shoulder. She carried him around with her always. She didn't know he was there, of course. But Charlie knew he was there.

Nick was spiky, pale yellow, very thin and long-drawn-out, with spiteful red eyes and a head the shape of a starfruit. He looked a lot like Jack Frost, except he was yellow. Charlie saw Jack Frost, too, but he didn't often admit it, even to himself. Jack Frost was the Spirit of Winter, of course, but Charlie didn't know that, until he met Nick as well. Then he began to understand. Everything had a spirit. *It was just that some people could see them*.

There were nice ones and nasty ones, of course. Charlie was clear about that. Nick was one spirit his mother could do without. He rode around on her neck most days and made her want to smoke more, and the more she smoked, the more spiteful he grew, the firmer and more spiky he appeared. He was pretty full of himself, the night Charlie Williams first spotted him when his mother was watching a film. The night he first saw Nick, Charlie Williams said: *'Wha- aa-tt?'*

His mother turned to look at him. Behind the smoke spiralling up from the ashtray on the arm of the settee, the Fifty-foot Woman strode through cities and brushed off tanks like gnats. 'What is it, Charlie?' his mother said. 'Charlie, are you all right?'

'Um, I don't know – what's *that*?'

'What's what?'

'Something – on your shoulder –'

Charlie's mother brushed her shoulder irritably. Charlie saw, with fascination, her hand pass *right through* Nick.

'Isn't it time you were in bed?'

'I am, I'm just –'

'What are you staring at?'

'You.'

'Have I grown a third eye, or something?'

She might as well have, Charlie thought. Instead, she'd grown a monster on her back. He'd come down to kiss his mother goodnight, when he saw, on her shoulder, a *thing*. The thing was the Spirit of Smoking. And it lived on his mother's back. Charlie watched, fascinated, as Nick curled his pale yellow tail around her neck. The pale yellow spikes running down his back rippled as she moved. He looked actually quite *heavy*, if spirits could ever weigh much. Charlie's mother didn't realise, but her shoulders were actually *bent*.

'A third eye?' Charlie said. 'No, I – you look strange.'

'I know, it's this make-up. I knew it was too dark when I bought it.' Charlie's mother lit a fresh cigarette. The Spirit of Nicotine winked. 'I knew I should have gone for Summer Shandy.'

'Summer Shandy?'

'Foundation. I haven't used much yet. I might take it back tomorrow. What are you waiting for? Come and kiss me goodnight.'

The Fifty-foot Woman crushed a few towns while Charlie struggled with himself. It took all Charlie's courage to kiss his mother goodnight, with the red-eyed Spirit of Nicotine in his face.

Charlie could smell him now. He smelt rank and bitter and greedy – greedy for power over his, Charlie's, mother and over anyone else he could sit on. He would never sit on Charlie. Charlie was wise to him, now.

''Night, then,' he said to his mother.

''Night, love,' she said, exhaling smoke.

Charlie went upstairs in a state of fear and confusion. *What other spirits were there?* He looked around his bedroom and the Spirit of Bedrooms was silent. He cleaned his teeth in the bathroom, and the Spirit of Toothpaste winked at him in the mirror. It looked a lot like him, with toothpaste round his mouth. He went back into his bedroom, and the Spirit of Cactus had written him a letter. He picked it up and read it: '**MORE WATER WHAT AM I DEAD?**'

Charlie watered his cactus. He felt sorry, now, that he'd neglected it. He felt sorry its rusty brown spirit had had to climb out of it to complain. Charlie filled a glass of water and set it beside his cactus. He wouldn't forget it again. Not now he'd seen its *spirit*.

He went to sleep in a whirl of clashing ideas. What would the Spirit of Water be like? The Spirit of Tea? Or Coffee? What about the Spirit of

Garlic? The Spirit of Gas Central Heating? Charlie thought about it, and he *knew* the Spirit of Petrol looked like Jarvis Cocker. It wore a jacket that shivered in rainbow colours, like petrol in a filling-station puddle, and it looked a bit seedy sometimes.

Charlie's mind raced. Would the Spirit of Chocolate be hot and exotic with Aztec feathers in its hair, or would it be cool and knowing? What would the Spirit of Alcohol look like? Or the Spirit of Cinema Popcorn? How about the Spirit of Bowling? Would the Spirit of Railway Stations have dust and crisp packets over it, or pigeons in its hair? What about Football? Would the Spirit of Tarmouth United be bulging with useful muscles, or would it look sickly and nerdish, since they'd just lost three games in a row? How about the Spirit of Pizza? Or the Spirit of Builders' Merchants? Pasties? Kippers? The Video Hire? *The Spirit of Fish and Chips?*

At last Charlie Williams felt the Spirit of Sleep and Dreams softly alight on his shoulders. In no time at all, he'd let it carry him away . . .

In the garden next morning, the Spirit of Runner Beans surprised him on top of the fence. It was long and red and it pulsed with lights.

Charlie saw it was *energy*. He'd never talked with a spirit before. He didn't know quite what to say.

'Hi,' he said, 'Runner Beans. I didn't know you could — I didn't, I mean — oh, this is *silly*.'

The spirit helped him out. It didn't talk at all. It simply sent him *growing* thoughts and glowed with manic energy. It filled him up completely, until he thought he'd grow or go mad. The runner-bean plants were growing, he saw, even as he watched them. Their tips swayed and felt for a hold on the fence, on sticks, on each other. Their brilliant scarlet flowers felt for bees. *Pollinate. Grow. Make beans.* This was all their spirit said. It was hard to think of anything else, so long as you watched them.

At last Charlie tore himself away, but he still felt like growing over breakfast. He sighed and stretched his toes.

'What's up with you this morning?' Charlie's mother stacked the dishwasher.

'I feel like — oh, I don't know.'

Charlie's mother looked at him. 'You're restless,' she said, 'like last night.'

'I know that,' Charlie acknowledged. 'It's just, I'm fed up with things.'

'What things?'

'I don't know. Things as they *are*.'

His father had gone out already, or he might have been able to tell him. Charlie got on well with his dad. He got on well with his mum, as well, but in a different way. Charlie's mother looked smart today. She worked behind the perfume counter in a glossy department store. Sometimes she brought perfumes home. Charlie knew all the names – Utopia, Excess, Renewal, Mantra, Psyche, Karisma! Today she smelled of Utopia. Charlie's mother sold a lot of Utopia. It was one of her most popular fragrances and a top niff in Charlie's book any day. Charlie thought he'd rush upstairs and smell the bottle and see what its spirit looked like. Probably she looked like a dream in silk, and her voice would be just like chocolate. The spirit of Utopia had to be a *babe*, if she looked the way Utopia smelt. Charlie was about to get up when his brother Warwick came in, smelling quite strongly of catfood.

'Stupid cat.' Warwick turned on the tap. 'Stupid cat's bowl tipped up, and I got it all over me – yuk.'

Warwick washed catfood off his hands. The Spirit of Catfood tried following him into the kitchen and got caught in the door behind him. It sicked up and spat and then melted away like a stain. Good job, Charlie thought. The Spirit of Catfood was a nightmare. He'd never seen anything like it. *A cat made of meat with forks and bones and dead things stuck all over it* – the Spirit of Catfood had to be the ugliest he'd seen.

Warwick towelled his hands disgustedly. He'd been feeding the cat in the garage, because Charlie never fed it, so *he* had to – something *else* he had to do that Charlie didn't. Warwick was younger than Charlie by two years, five months and twenty-one days, which made Charlie the boss of Warwick by a not inconsiderable margin. Another thing which made him the boss of Warwick was that Charlie could remember all the stupid things he'd done, like the time Warwick had got lost in Denham's department store, when he'd gone in with Mum when he was little, when she'd only just started her job.

'Remember the time you got lost in Denham's with Mum?' Charlie said, enjoying the Spirit of Warwick, which looked like Warwick, aged four.

'No,' Warwick said. 'Remind me, why don't you? I've only heard it half a million times.'

'Remember you hid in the luggage department? And then you followed Mum? But it wasn't Mum at all, it was —'

'Some other woman, ha, ha.' Warwick picked up his schoolbag. 'I'm going now. Coming, or what?'

Or what, Charlie thought, was his preferred option today. Who wanted to go to school, with the world so *spirited* and flavourful? No way, he'd like to have said. I've got things to *see*.

'Come on, then,' Warwick said, crossly. 'We better go some time this *century*.'

It was no use. He'd have to go to school now, Charlie could see. It wouldn't matter what he said. What wonderful things he could see. *Please, sir. I saw the Spirit of Runner Beans and the Spirit of Catfood this morning. Can I have the day off to see the Spirit of Everything Else?* He couldn't see it going down too well. So he couldn't go into town today; that didn't stop him wanting to. Charlie burned to see the Spirit of Shopping Malls, the Spirit of Sportswear, Surf-shops, Piers, Pavilions, Arcade Games, Bus Stations, Fountains, Country Fried Chicken, HMV Records, Smith's, Woollies, Boots — the Spirit of *Everything*. A whole world waited out there. But it would have to wait a bit longer. Today he would have to settle for the Spirit of

German Grammar, probably some seventy-year-old milkmaid who got very cross when you spoke. Or maybe the Spirit of Maths, a jumble of sharp, mixed-up numbers. Or Art, which looked like Van Gogh.

''Bye, Mum,' Charlie said. 'We're going now.' Then he said, 'Mum, I know it's hard, but – I *wish* you'd give up smoking.'

Charlie's mother looked at him. Nick glared down at him redly from her neck. He raised his spines a little. He showed his yellow teeth. Better not upset him, Charlie thought. He doesn't want me to say that, Charlie thought. Who knows what he might do?

'Did you take some dinner money, Charlie?' Charlie's mother stood by the door and applied her final lipstick.

'Mum, did you hear what I said?'

'I wish, too,' she said, sadly. 'Have a good day now, won't you?'

Charlie kissed his mother goodbye and smelled Nick's nicotine breath. Nick's grip on his mother had tightened, Charlie knew. It would grow tighter still at work with every coffee-break. He hated to leave his mother with Nick round her neck all day. Why couldn't Nick get off her back? Why couldn't he, Charlie, save her? The Spirit of Nicotine read his thoughts. It crackled threateningly when it moved. But only Charlie could hear it. Better not upset him, Charlie thought.

He couldn't dislodge Nick, Charlie knew. Not without some help.

'That's the spirit,' Charlie's dad said. 'Well done, Charlie boy.'

His mother had gone out of the room leaving her smoking ashtray for a moment. Charlie had stubbed out her cigarette and hidden it under the table. He wouldn't be too popular when she got back. But Dad was behind him, at least.

'Mum won't like it,' Charlie said. 'She's told me off already.'

'Get over it, Charlie,' she'd told him. 'I know what you're trying to do, but it's just annoying, all right?'

'Never you mind, Charlie boy,' Dad said. 'Let's hope she gets the message.'

Charlie had been sending his mother plenty of messages lately. He had, in fact, launched his Stub It campaign a week ago last Tuesday. Something had to be done. Nick had got fat and complacent. He lay around Charlie's mother's neck with his pale yellow tail hanging down. It looked grotesque. She didn't know – how could she? On Saturdays Nick ballooned overnight, when Charlie's parents met friends at the pub and stayed to talk for hours. Sundays, he took it easy. His body grew heavier, yellower. His death-breath stank of furnaces and ashtrays, of frightful bitter acids and acrid things that ate away your stomach. He'd taken to winking at Charlie over meals and trying to inch his tail over Charlie's neck, so that Charlie found himself wondering what cigarettes actually *tasted* like. He'd almost caught himself tasting one. It had happened one night last week.

One night the previous week – Monday night, it was – Charlie had been doing his homework in the middle of the kitchen table, when he'd felt a touch on his neck. He looked up. Nothing but the Spirit of Homework, he thought morosely. But the miserable-looking Spirit of Homework had pulled up a pew and lost itself in its knitting. In its place stood the Spirit of Nicotine, crackling ever-so-slightly.

'Get away from me,' Charlie said. 'You stink.'

'Don't be like that,' Nick wheedled. 'You owe me, am I wrong?'

'I *owe* you? I don't *think* so.'

'I let you see everything.'

'You did? You mean,' Charlie lowered his voice, 'the *spirits* of everything?'

'That's right,' said the Spirit of Nicotine. 'And the least you can do is try me.'

His mother's packet of cigarettes lay on the kitchen table.

Charlie balked. 'As if.'

'Go on,' Nick wheedled, 'taste one.'

'So you can sit on my neck?'

'I could sit on your neck anyway.'

'No,' Charlie said, 'you couldn't.'

Nick's eyes glowed. 'I could *try*.'

Charlie got up and opened a can of beans. 'What other spirits are there?' he said. 'I want to know them *all*.'

'Oh, there's lots,' Nick said, putting his feet up. 'As many as you like.'

'How come I never saw them before?'

'Have you ever *looked*?'

Baked beans in a bowl with fingers of bread was a favourite with Charlie for supper. He got out a pan and heated his beans and thought about ways to trap Nick. It wasn't going to be easy to outwit him. How *did* you get rid of an unwelcome spirit? A spirit as *well in* as Nick?

'Did you try giving him a taste of his own medicine?' the Spirit of Baked Beans enquired.

Charlie dropped his spoon in the pan. '*What* did you say?' he said.

'Him. Old Nick.' The Spirit of Baked Beans fished out Charlie's spoon and licked its fingers. It looked like a big fat baby dressed in orange. 'He's a nasty piece of work, he is. Did you try giving him a taste of a spirit *he doesn't like*?'

'Excuse me?' Nick said to it, smartly. '*Should* you be sitting on a work surface next to a cooker?'

'Don't try that with *me*.' The Spirit of Baked Beans flicked hot beans at Nick. 'I know what *your* game is.'

Charlie whipped the pan away and poured beans into his bowl. The Spirit of Baked Beans chatted until he'd eaten them. Then it had had to go. Something to do with a meeting. In some transport café.

'So who don't you like?' Charlie said.

'Hoo,' Nick said, 'hoo, hoo.'

'Between you and me,' Charlie said.

'Between you and me, I'd like a smoke.'

Suddenly Charlie saw. His only power over Nick lay in *what Nick wanted him to do*.

'So would I,' Charlie said. Charlie took out a cigarette and put it into his mouth.

'Go on,' Nick wheedled, 'light up.'

Charlie flicked the lighter. A little flame jumped up. Spirits of Smoke and Fire fizzed and whispered in his ears.

'Try me,' Nick wheedled. 'Where's the big deal?'

'I may,' Charlie said. 'I just might. But which *is* your least favourite spirit?'

The lighter flame danced in Nick's eye. He hissed and made a circle on the table. His pale yellow triangular spines quivered with the desire for Charlie to light up. Round and round he circled. Suddenly, back he came in Charlie's face. 'I don't care for that smell in the garage.'

'What smell?'

'That *mess* called the Spirit of Catfood.' Nick shuddered. 'It has no style. It's savage.'

'I'm not crazy about it, either.'

'Fine tobacco and *catfood* – ugh. The very thought. It's revolting.'

Charlie brought the lighter close, then closer. Then he laid it down. 'I don't think I will, after all.'

'*You don't know what you're missing!*' Nick hissed, circling angrily on the table.

'Oh,' Charlie said, 'I think I do.'

That had been more than a week ago. Since then, the Stub It campaign had taken considerable risks. Nick was dangerous, Charlie knew. But stubbing out her cigarettes was making his mother cross. It was helping Nick win her over. Thoroughly at home by now on Charlie's mother's back, Nick cleaned his claws in Charlie's face. He clicked and coiled his tail. He winked and blinked his eyes. He made Charlie's mother frantic if she thought the shops had closed. No matter how much Utopia she sprayed on at work, Charlie's mum always smelled of Nick. He made her short of breath on stairs. Get up, whenever he wanted. And the larger Nick grew, the more bent and worried she looked.

Charlie's mother had to do whatever Nick wanted, and there was nothing Charlie could do about it. Nick lay and blinked at him nightly. *Easy — ea-sy — ea-sy.*

He was fighting a losing battle. Warwick knew it. Charlie's dad knew it. Dibley the *cat* knew it. The worst of it was, so did Charlie. Charlie exchanged a look with his dad as his mother re-entered the room. Wait for it, Charlie thought.

'Charlie, where's that cigarette?' she demanded.

'It went out,' Charlie said.

'No, it didn't. You stubbed it out. You'll have to get off this, Charlie.'

Nick grinned wolfishly over Charlie's mother's shoulder. Charlie felt depressed. He wasn't supernatural, was he? How could he fight a sprite? How could he hope to win? He found his mother's jumper over the chair, the jumper she wore round her shoulders to watch TV – the monkey jumper, they called it, because it was woolly and brown and huge and made of matted mohair. He might as well sit in the monkey jumper as try to explain how he *felt*. He pulled it on and sat in it, but *even the monkey jumper smelled of Nick*. Its spirit looked just like a monkey. It sat on Charlie and grinned. Charlie pushed it off. This was getting stupid. What next? The Spirit of Tea-towels?

Warwick came in with a very full glass of orange juice and set it down gingerly on the table. The cat slipped in behind him and began to wash itself. Warwick smelled vaguely of catfood. The Spirit of Catfood tried following him in round the door, but as usual it had trouble with the sticks and forks and fish-heads and lids of catfood tins that stuck out all over it, like lumps in a Christmas pudding. *A cat made of meat with dead things stuck in it.* It looked like a badly made bird's nest, with a big, jowly cat in the middle, except that it smelt a lot worse. It had eyes like a fish, fishbones for whiskers and a loose, mealy mouth with forgotten bits of meat hanging out of it. Wherever it went, it carried its own cloud of flies. Poo – *yuck*, Charlie thought. He watched in fascination as the Spirit of Catfood nudged its way in round the door. Little did Warwick know he had a friend.

Why couldn't Charlie get smelly sometimes? Taking the tops off catfood. Right after breakfast and dinner. It made him want to *hurl*. Warwick kicked the door shut, annoyed. 'Stupid cat's always leaving the door open.'

'Possibly you are,' Dad said.

The Spirit of Catfood belched and let out a gas.

'Pooh!' Warwick held his nose. 'Put Dibsy out, someone, will you?'

Warwick meant Dibley the cat. Warwick had named the cat after the cat in *Red Dwarf*, which had been changed into nerdy Duane Dibley, but no one ever called it by its name. Mostly they called it Catface or Smell or Junkfood, because that was what it ate. Charlie picked up the cat and put it out in the garden. He watched it wander off into the runner beans. The Spirits of Evening are *abroad*, he found himself thinking. Then he went back inside.

'What's that on your shoulder?' he suddenly asked Warwick.

Warwick looked up. 'What?'

'That – spiky thing. Keep still.'

It was nothing at all. Charlie tried, but he couldn't pick it up. It had looked like a spike – a triangular, pale yellow spike – which had melted away as he touched it and left a suspicious smell.

'You been smoking?' Charlie asked.

Warwick snorted. '*Would* I?'

Maybe, Charlie thought. If Nick got a foot on your shoulder. That's *it*, Charlie thought, that really is. That's just about the *end*.

That night, he got up at midnight. He got dressed and went into town. The glorious Spirits of Evening were abroad in carefree bands, swaggering in the side-streets and spilling out of clubs. They danced in the lights of the bandstand and all along the sea-front. The sea lapped Charlie's feet as he walked along the sand. It didn't care if it lapped his feet, or if it didn't. It didn't care about anything, and its spirit was too big and boundless to be seen or understood, at least by the likes of himself. Charlie turned back towards town.

The town led him on and on and Charlie followed. He walked the greasy late-night streets and a sad young man in a sleeping bag asked him for money. Charlie gave him all he had, but the young man hardly noticed. Charlie walked in the park and the Spirits of Roses and Japonica soothed him as he passed. He passed the aviaries in the Pleasure Gardens, and the hot-eyed Spirits of Parrots followed him as he went.

Charlie danced in fountains. He ran through glittering arcades. He window-shopped for his wish-list, and the Spirits of Reebok and Nike came to join him. Charlie ran on, through streets filled with girls in short dresses who linked arms and shouted at taxis and giggled and fell off their shoes. Charlie could see their high spirits. They looked like fizzy fireworks or popping neon balloons. They were pretty funny to watch. A few girls, Charlie noticed, had mini-Nicks on their shoulders. He hoped they wouldn't get weighed down. They looked so bright and bubbly.

Charlie ran on and on. The Spirits of Fishes depressed him, hunting and sucking the walls in the dark aquarium, but the Spirit of Kingburger filled him up and sent him on his way. Low spirits, high spirits, cut-price spirits, impossible spirits – Charlie Williams saw them all. Best of all – he saw it in the shop windows as it flitted from pane to pane – he thought he saw *the Spirit of Charlie Williams*.

When Charlie Williams got home his world was teeming. More and more spirits of more and more things thronged his mind and clamoured for his attention. They filled the garden. They filled the house. He could hardly get in at the door.

This is stupid, Charlie thought. He'd thought he'd have a snack but he couldn't even sit *down*. The Spirit of Breakfast Cereal, the Spirit of Butter and Sugar, of Bowls and Plates and Spoons – they sat in the chairs, they were in the fridge, the cupboards, they were even in the *oven*, he could see them through the door. Charlie got in a panic. He held his head. He went upstairs. The Spirit of Teeth, the Spirit of Maths, the Spirit of his Pencil-case, the Spirit of his own Jumper –

'STOP!' Charlie cried. '*ENOUGH!*'

'Enough?' said Nick. 'But Charlie, we've only just started.'

'What do you mean?' Charlie said. 'You can get off my bed *right now*.'

'Oh,' Nick said, 'I don't think so.' And he crossed his legs with a scraping sound. 'Unless, of course, you really have seen enough?'

'That's what I said, didn't I?' Charlie was pretty upset. 'I want you to go away. And take all these other ones *with* you.'

'Well, now,' Nick said smoothly, 'I can't do what you say, unless, of course, you –'

'Try me? No *way*!' Charlie said. 'I'll never get rid of you, *unless* –'

Charlie raced downstairs to the darkened garage. He flipped on the light. *There* – stacks of Dibsy's catfood, in little tins with ringpulls. Plaice and Cod. Beef with Heart. Duck with Turkey. Turkey with Chicken. Chicken with Game. Game with Rabbit. Rabbit with Liver and Gravy. Which would be the smelliest? he wondered. Probably Plaice and Cod. You couldn't beat fish for smells. And smells were what he wanted. Quickly pulling a ringpull, he forked Plaice and Cod Chunks with Extra Vitamins for Strong Teeth and a Glossy Coat into Dibsy's smelliest bowl. He paused and listened. Now what? 'Come on, then,' he said. He turned off the light. *'Come on, then. I know you're there.'*

Charlie waited. The Spirit of Catfood sneezed

and got up heavily. It wheezed a bit as it walked, and bits of meat fell off it and melted away. Charlie darted up the stairs. He waved his bowl. *Come on.*

Up in Charlie's bedroom, Nick lit a fresh cigarette. The smoke curled up in spirals and settled over Charlie Williams's things. His mother would think he'd been smoking, even though he hadn't, even though he *would*, before too long. Soon he would get the taste for it. It was only a matter of time.

'No sense in hiding, Charlie.' Nick tapped ash on the floor. 'Charlie, is that you?'

The door swung back. Instead of Charlie Williams, the nightmare Spirit of Catfood stood in the door. It sneezed a few times. It didn't like smoke. It didn't like smoke at *all*.

'Now, Charlie,' Nick said, 'let's talk about this –'

The Spirit of Catfood growled.

'After all,' Nick said, 'your mother can't do without me.'

The Spirit of Catfood hissed and raised its hackles.

'Charlie,' Nick said, 'I thought we were *friends*.' And he drew in his pale yellow tail.

'What gave you that idea?'

Charlie threw his smelly fork. The Spirit of Catfood sprang. Sticks and flies and rotting meat flew off it in all directions. Nick yowled and howled and stretched himself out into thin yellow smoke and wafted away down the stairwell. The Spirit of Catfood gave chase, well up the garden and down the road, and down the *next* road after that. Charlie Williams listened. Yowling. And howling. Fading away. Then nothing. Then peace and quiet.

It would come back when it had finished, Charlie supposed. He pictured the Spirit of Catfood surprising the postman. Or maybe it wouldn't. Charlie looked around his quiet room. He looked in vain for the Spirit of Maths or Teeth, or the Spirit of Prickly Cactus. In vain for the Spirit of Everything. The spirits, that night, were still.

Hi, this is Charlie. I'm actually forty-two, now. I wrote this story, about the time we had Nick in the house, because I see Nick now and then on someone's shoulder, and I really think they should know what old Red-eye's *like*. These are old memories now. This is actually a story about my brother, know why? I don't mean Warwick — well, I'll tell you.

Nick

Around the time I set the Spirit of Catfood on Nick and it drove him away – I'm remembering now, from a long time ago, but it seemed just about the same time – my mother got sick every morning. 'I don't feel like smoking or eating,' she said. 'I feel really sick in the mornings.'

She never smoked ever again. And seven or eight months after that, my new baby brother was born. I begged them not to. But they did it anyway. My new baby brother – that's right – they called him *Nick*.

Stupid Cows

There was once a cow called Wisdom.

'Hey, Wisdom, what's new?' Jamie said.

Wisdom crossed the mud-filled yard. Her hoofs stuck with every step. She put her face on the wall. Jamie tickled it a bit.

It hadn't always been this way. It hadn't been this way very long.

Jamie Sleep never *had* liked cows. Especially the cows down the road. Whenever he walked the dog past the farm they watched him very closely. The way they followed his every move with steady concentration had always seemed a bit, well, *sinister*, somehow. Jamie guessed they were pretty good at pretending they were just a bunch of cows standing around in the muck, steaming and blowing, not thinking anything in particular. But Jamie Sleep knew better.

At home, he said, 'Cows are sneaky.'

'Sneaky?' Jamie's father looked at him. 'Sneaky? What do you mean?'

'The way they stare at you when you walk past. I mean, like, what are they thinking?'

'Thinking? Cows don't *think*.'

'They do,' Jamie said. 'It's just, they pretend they don't.'

Jamie's dad folded the paper. 'And why would they do that?'

'They don't want us to *know*, of course. But when you turn round, they're watching.'

The cows watched Jamie, whether he ambled or ran past their yard. Whether he ignored them or booed them. Whether he tried to understand them, or whether he didn't. What were they thinking? Why did he always feel *guilty* whenever he passed them? Did they know something he didn't know? Didn't they know it was rude to stare or go to the toilet in public? Did they *talk* about him after he was gone?

These and other questions bothered Jamie Sleep. The cows down the road had hidden depths, he felt sure. It couldn't be just as simple as standing around in the muck. Not the way those eyes looked. Those eyes that followed you around. It took him a very long time to find out they weren't really sinister at all. But still he didn't trust them. Neither did Jamie's dog Kip.

Jamie Sleep's dog Kip had always growled at the cows down the road, every time she passed them. But after he saw a programme on telly about a vet moving one of a cow's *four stomachs* back into place by tipping her on her back and kneading it over, Jamie began to feel differently. 'Cows have four stomachs, right, because one stomach isn't enough,' Jamie explained to his mother.

'Isn't it, love?' his mother commented, absently.

'Know why?'

'Why what?'

'Why cows have four stomachs.'

'Because grass is hard to digest?'

'Yes, well, sort of.' Jamie felt deflated. The news that cows had four stomachs had seemed pretty sensational to *him*. 'But I bet you don't know what they're called.'

'Stomachs one to four?'

'What happens is,' Jamie said, 'they have to chew grass down, right? Then they have to digest it. First it goes into stomach one. Then – get this – they sick it up and *chew it all over again*. Gross, or what?'

'Gross,' Jamie's mother agreed.

'Then it's called the cud. The cud goes to stomach two, right, which *actually has little stones in it* to pulp it up some more, then it goes to the next one, and the next. The fourth stomach's, like, the *real* stomach, called the am–something, I think. The rest are only food blenders for mixing up sick made of grass. Sounds pretty yuk, right? But cows do it *all the time*.'

'Good job you don't have four stomachs.'

'Diseases of cows are pretty yuk, too,' Jamie went on earnestly. 'You should hear what they get – displaced stomach, infected udders, TB, worms, BSE . . .'

'Poor cows,' said Jamie's mum.

Jamie Sleep began to visit the cows down the road. They didn't *look* like they had four stomachs. They looked like they could do with some fresh straw to sleep on. Were they *meant* to be standing in poo all the time? Didn't cows get foot-rot? Jamie felt sure, if *he* was a cow, he wouldn't like never being mucked out and having no fresh straw, like the cows down the road never had. Week in, week out, Jamie and Kip went by and the muck in the cow-shed never changed. No new straw went down on top of the old. There *was* no straw. The cows simply slept on mud – soggy, churned-up mud and cow-pats, that was what they slept on. And the farmer never came to see to them, or if he did, he didn't care.

The cows didn't shout about it. They simply stood and stared. Or they ripped out silage from their metal silage cage in the middle of all that muck and munched it up *meaningfully* and nodded and stared at Jamie, so that he actually felt uncomfortable, like something was down to *him*. The munching wasn't the problem. It was the *staring* Jamie didn't like.

The cows down the road really got to Jamie Sleep. He got so he wouldn't pass them. Then he got so he ran past them really quickly. Then he tried stopping and offering them grass, but found he was actually trembling. Then he got really fed up. He wouldn't be scared of *cows*.

One day they all got out. "Twas on account of the election, see?' as Farmer Willis put it. "Twould never've happened, else.'

The day they escaped and trod all over the village, the cows were peacefully trooping from field to shed in the lane when the Wilfred Destry Election Special came round the corner and frightened them out of their wits. Wilfred Destry's van split the herd in two halves and put several cows in the hedge. Wilfred Destry's fluttering orange election banners did for the rest of them. Wilfred Destry's voice boomed out. His megaphone drove them mad. 'VOTE DESTRY,' it said, in a voice the size of two counties. 'YOUR LOCAL MAN FOR LOCAL REPRE-SENTATION.'

By the time the Election Special had zoomed off up the lane, half the cows had scattered in people's gardens. The rest of them had bolted around the village in terror and confusion, rub-bishing drives and planters, kicking up shrubs and fences, getting tangled in washing lines and hopelessly trapped in carports – and all because of Wilf Destry's election pledges and Wilf Destry's election van with its hugely booming megaphone on top.

Jamie Sleep had been reading comics that Saturday. He heard the Election Special roaring off up the road. 'DESTRY RIDES AGAIN . . . I HOPE I CAN COUNT ON YOUR VOTE . . .' He heard a surge of heavy hoofs in the lane, shouts and whoops, the sound of splintering wood.

Then he heard his father scream with rage. *'What-about-this-mess?'* he heard him shouting. *'You come back, d'you hear?'*

Jamie Sleep jumped up and ran outside. What did he see but *cows*. His father, shouting at cows. Cows skidding around in the garden, up to their fetlocks, or whatever they were, in his father's treasured lawn. Cows lowing in panic, not know-ing which way to turn. Cows disappearing up the lane, one or two of them in skirts and blouses and other streaming articles of other people's washing. One cow, in particular, flopping down off the garden with what looked like *tights* on her head.

'What's happening?' Jamie said.

'We're having a party, can't you see? *Oi!*' shouted Jamie's father, as Farmer Willis rattled by in his muck-covered tractor. *'Can't you keep your cows in? What about my lawn?'*

Farmer Willis nodded and smiled and tore off up the lane after his cattle. He didn't look too happy. Neither did Jamie Sleep, after his father surveyed the garden.

'Well, thank you, Farmer Willis. I wanted holes in my lawn.'

'They couldn't help it,' Jamie said. 'Probably they were frightened.'

Stupid Cows

'Pestering cows,' Jamie's father said. 'Pestering *hoof*-marks all over the place.'

'Wonder what scared 'em?'

'That idiot Wilfred Destry can't have helped.' Morosely Jamie's father counted the clop-holes — as Jamie soon christened them — in his mowed and treasured grass where Farmer Willis's cows had done a tango. 'They've made a mess of it,' he said. 'We'll need to fill in all these holes.'

'Why can't Debs do it?' Jamie meant his sister.

'Because I'm asking *you*.'

Jamie Sleep felt less than friendly towards cows in general, and Wilfred Destry's election effort in particular, after a staggeringly dull Saturday afternoon spent filling in clop-holes in the lawn with a mixture of sand and compost — surprisingly deep holes, as it turned out. The cows up the village were soon rounded up, as it happened, and returned to their mucky home-from-home down the road, minus other people's socks and pants and trousers, and the village assessed the damage and grumbled quite a bit for a day or two, and then it all blew over. These things happen, after all. It wasn't as if it was the cows' fault. As Farmer Willis himself said, 'That there Wilfred Destry, he would've waked the dead.'

The cows down the road took a dim view of Wilfred Destry. He didn't get their vote. Jamie Sleep knew, because they told him. They told him quite a few things, once he bothered to listen.

'How's things?' he often asked them.

'OK,' they said. 'Could be better. The cow-cake's pretty crummy these days.'

'I'm sorry,' said Jamie. 'Anything else?'

'We'd like more room in our sheds, please. Plus we'd like a scratching post and something to *do*.'

'Is that it?' Jamie said.

'That's only the start,' they said darkly.

'You're cows,' Jamie said, 'that's the way that it is. And you know Wilf Destry's van?'

'We don't like Wilf Destry's van. We don't even like Wilf Destry.'

'I can see why,' Jamie said. 'But there's going to be an *election*. An election's where you change things, if you want.'

The cows nodded moodily, Jamie thought. He guessed they felt left out. After they'd done the dance on his dad's lawn and worn the village washing, Jamie thought he knew what the cows down the road were thinking. He got quite fascinated with them. He and Kip watched them most days when they went for a walk — and they went for a walk together most days, before Jamie went to school. They weren't nearly as daft as they looked, he thought. Not by a long chalk, he thought. Kip didn't understand them. She didn't understand their clouded, purple-brown eyes, which held the depth of the world in their reflection, but didn't like to let on.

But after a while, Jamie Sleep did. He liked nothing better than to rest his elbows on the concrete-block wall bordering the shippen, or cow-house, and put his chin in his hands and consider the four different sides of their world — a dung-filled yard bordered on three sides by yawning agricultural sheds, which clanged in the winds rolling up from the valley, and on the fourth by the wall he often sat on. The cows didn't mind him watching them. But Jamie minded for them. Didn't they *know* what happened to milkers over nine or ten years old? Didn't they *mind* a comfortless shed? He knew they did, because they'd told him. But had they told anyone else? Didn't they *know* an election was coming? *Wasn't it time they spoke out?*

Jamie looked into their eyes. What *was* it about patient cows? They didn't mope. They didn't worry about the future. They simply chewed silage and waited. They'd been around a long time, he guessed. They weren't in any hurry.

Jamie tried again to hold out some grass. 'Come on, then,' he said. 'You know you like it.'

One cow, in particular, had always helped Jamie when he forced himself to hold grass out and not get scared. It was always the cow with the white map of Africa on her forehead – the cow who led the others, Jamie noticed, so she'd be *queen* of the herd. Gently probing and belching, she came forward now and hoovered up Jamie's grass with a rasp of her dead-looking tongue.

'No need to burp,' Jamie said. 'You're not so bad, are you? Even if you *are* pretty filthy.' And he scratched the queen cow's nose and she stood and let him, and it came to him that her name was Wisdom. 'You shouldn't stand in all this mud. Watch out, or your feet'll rot.'

Jamie wondered aloud how their feet didn't rot, standing in all that manure. 'Seen your coat lately?' he scolded. 'It's filthy. Stiff with bobbles – bobbles of mud. Don't you ever *wash*?'

And the cows looked at him patiently, and the more Jamie looked, the more the clouds in their eyes seemed to say, 'We're thinking – can't you see?' Huffing and hooshing like hair-dryers, tails switching, ears twitching –

they all drew close and one of them *pooed* – 'Yuk!' Jamie held his nose. 'You *stink*!'

The cows didn't mind. They didn't mind Jamie. They didn't mind each other. They didn't mind the smell. They didn't mind anything at all, except – no one ever asked them their *opinion*. Ever. Not even in election year.

A man and a dog walked past. Jamie watched them approaching. He guessed the man wouldn't say hello. Sometimes people didn't, he didn't know why. Jamie waited. A cow screeched, somewhere in the shed. They did that, sometimes – probably tummy-ache. There came a moment when the man with the dog might have said, 'Nice morning,' then the man and the dog walked on. *His loss*, Jamie thought. Jamie winked at the cows. They don't know what *we* know, do they?

And the cows munched silage meaningfully and Jamie knew they wouldn't let on. And, from that moment, Jamie understood them. And he took it upon himself to act as – their *spokesman*, I suppose.

A rasping blue tongue on his arm reminded him where he was. Plus the slap of falling dung.

'You've got no manners,' Jamie said. 'You're really very *rude*.'

And he said goodbye, and walked away – and the cows put their faces on the wall and watched him go, until he couldn't see them any more. He looked back again and again. Beasts of the field, he thought. Or beasts of the plop-heap, more like. They weren't very beastly, at all – and he thought of the clouds in their eyes. And their ears – it hurt him to look at the tags in their ears. They were sensitive, pink – ears like yours and mine. It had hurt them – *ow!* – when the tag had been punched in.

But still they hadn't complained.

'Perhaps they haven't complained before because things've been all right up to now,' Jamie's father joked.

'Steak Nite *upsets* them,' Jamie insisted. 'They want the signs taken down.'

'They do, do they?' Jamie's dad raised his eyebrows in a whimsical way Jamie hated. 'Would they like a Whist Drive instead? How will they know the difference?'

Jamie Sleep sighed. Passing things on from a cow's point of view wasn't ever going to be easy.

But Dad was only the half of it. No one took the bovine view seriously, least of all the publican up at the Crow's Nest, who'd upset cows for miles around with his tactless Steak Nite sign, right on the opposite side of the road to a herd of impressionable bullocks. SERIOUS STEAKS FROM £3.99 A HEAD, said the sign. ELECTION SUPPER FOURTH OF MAY.

'Okay,' Jamie said, 'so they can't read. *But they know the smell of a well-done steak when it's cooking.*'

Jamie kept the cows up the road well informed. He'd go up the road with the *West Country Clarion* and read to them in a stern voice, glancing up every now and then to make sure they were taking it in. They always were. Information-starved, or what? They were mad for a bit of local goss to break the monotony of the cowshed. Usually the high points of their day were their six o'clock and four o'clock dates with the milking parlour, where they at least got to listen to Radio One plus national traffic reports over the muck-splattered old tranny in the eaves.

But the papers were something new. Sometimes the cows drew so close that the *West Country Clarion* grew warm in the circle of their interested breath. Once or twice they'd got carried away and put out a blue tongue to eat it, but Jamie had pressed on, regardless. They always went quiet when he read them the television schedules. He took to reading them 'This Week at the Sales' against the boom and bong of the wind-sucked sides of the sheds. The cows listened patiently as Jamie read out stock prices:' "Sales of calves only eight weeks old were fetching rock-bottom prices. They didn't make sixty pounds. Many were withdrawn from sale at the Bastable markets." ' Then he wondered. What was he *doing* reading out prices for calves? Wasn't it pretty tactless, not to say upsetting?

He'd tried to pick something relating to cattle, that was all. Instead, he moved on to read them the front-page news. The papers were full of the coming election, so Jamie read polls and profiles, reports of visiting dignitaries, expected voting statistics, likely swings, burning issues, local margins for victory, effects of the common agricultural policy. The cows lowed once or twice when he mentioned live exports and milk quotas, so he read them those bits again. He even read local candidate Wilf Destry's life story, plus Things I Would Do If Elected. He wasn't bad on animal rights. In fact, he was pretty solid.

'Get this,' Jamie said. He put on his best reading voice: ' "Most people, Destry believes, would be prepared to pay a bit more," ' Jamie lowered his voice,' "for meat," 'louder again' "to see farm animals better treated." That's good, isn't it?' He looked up. The nearest cow thoughtfully tried to eat his sleeve. Another belched somewhere. Jamie put the paper away. He thought the rest looked interested.

In comparison with the other candidates standing, Wilf had quite a bit going for him. The main thing *not* in his favour was that he drove too fast. To make things fair Jamie read out articles on each of the other candidates, so that the cows could weigh the issues. By the time he'd finished he knew quite a bit about it, and so, he hoped, did the cows. At least, they hadn't *said* that they'd been bored.

With barely a week to go before the election, Jamie – and the cows – had had time to think. They were absorbed, now, whenever he and Kip went down the road. Heads together over their silage, they merely switched their tails and nodded politely when Jamie and Kip went by, then continued their line of debate. The election had given them a subject for discussion. *Someone had asked them their opinion!* Even their back ends looked serious. Jamie knew they were thinking hard. Thinking was what they did best.

At dinner that night, Jamie's father cut up his pasty and put on *Election Preview*.

'And a troubled day for local candidate Wilfred Destry in a triple vehicle pile-up in sleepy South Moldbury...' announced the presenter, over pictures of crashed cars in Moldbury.

The troubled face of Destry replaced the cars – a ruddy face with tawny hair and eyebrows. Jamie Sleep sat up. It was the first time he'd seen Wilfred Destry.

'How bad *was* the crash?' the interviewer asked.

'Well, you know...' Wilf Destry smiled. His tawny eyebrows rose. He had a lazy way of rolling out his words, as if what they *meant* didn't matter so much as his *smile*. 'Well, you know, Denzil, these things have a way of getting exaggerated, don't they?'

'You *did* overturn,' Denzil said.

'Well, we've minor damage, but that's to be expected in any slight collision.'

'And you *did* almost kill three horses. Not a very good election message, is it?'

'Well, now, Denzil, with our country lanes so narrow, unfortunately these things will happen. I mean to say, I —'

'And the Destry Election Special ended up in a hedge, I understand?'

'I'm continuing my campaign on foot.' Wilfred Destry smiled, and his rich voice poured out like treacle. 'I'll be out and about, talking to farmers this week, targeting those issues like —'

'Speed limits?'

'Those issues that matter to *farmers* and the farming community.'

'That's all we've got time for, I'm afraid.'

Wilfred Destry disappeared and Jamie lost interest. The report on local issues bumbled on in the background while Jamie ate his tea. His sister Debs spent some time complaining bitterly about having to *sign out* at lunchtime at school (Why should I? What am I? Six years old?) but Jamie only listened with half an ear, remembering the day of the clop-holes, the day the cows had run riot, scattered by Wilfred Destry and his speeding Election-mobile. But no more. The Destry Election Special had gone belly up in South Moldbury. Cows of the world, rejoice. *Destry had crashed in the hedge.*

'Why do I *have* to sign out?' Debs complained. 'What do they think? I'm going to run away and not come back?'

'It's just a formality,' Dad rumbled. 'Not too much trouble, is it?'

'It makes you feel they don't trust you. Plus when you come back you have to show your sixth-form identity card to even get *in*? Plus reception's locked up like a *prison*.'

'It's for your own benefit, I expect.'

'The cows don't agree,' Jamie said.

'What's that?' His father looked up.

'The cows down the road. They say it's a shame. They say we should all take time to think about what it *means*.'

'What what means?'

'To feel free to go where you want. And not have tags in your ears.'

'They do, do they?'

'What's important to them is a government strong on animal rights. What's important to them is –'

'I'm not hearing this – the cows down the road – talk *politics*?'

'They like music, as well,' Jamie said. 'They listen to Radio One when they're being milked.'

Jamie Sleep's father set down his knife and fork. Then he began to laugh. He laughed until he choked on his pasty. He had to be banged on the back. Then he laughed some more.

'You can laugh,' Jamie said, severely. 'It's all right for you. You can laugh all you want while you're *eating* 'em.'

'You are funny, Jamie,' Jamie's mother said. 'Isn't he funny, Debs?'

'Hilarious,' Debs agreed.

'This election,' Jamie went on. 'What they want to know is, what's in it for them? Will conditions improve for cows? That's what they want to know.'

Jamie's dad wiped his eyes. 'What, are they *voting* now?'

'They'd like to,' Jamie said earnestly. 'They'd like to do lots of things.'

'Perhaps they'd like to go windsurfing?'

'No,' Jamie said, 'don't be silly. But there's other things they could do.'

'Such as?'

'They don't complain much,' Jamie said. 'They make the best of things. And they're really patient. I think they could teach us a lot.'

'You do, do you?'

'Yes,' Jamie said, 'I do. They say we're too busy. We shouldn't hurry so much.'

'We shouldn't hurry.'

'They never do. That's what makes them so patient. They have plenty of time to *think*.'

Jamie's dad got up. 'Cows. Time to think. This is silly,' he said. 'I've got things to *do*. Not talk about flaming *cows*.'

All that week the election posters went up. VOTE DESTRY, YOUR LOCAL CANDI- DATE, they blared from hedges and sign-posts, shops and village noticeboards, from telegraph poles and gate-posts, over fields of indifferent sheep. And all that week, on and off, Jamie kept his dad up to speed on the cows' latest plans. They had *big* plans now that they'd decided, at last, which candidate they'd support.

'You know Wilf Destry crashed his van the other day,' Jamie told them. 'He only ran down three horses and almost killed them.'

'We know,' the cows said. 'He came here.'

'Wilfred Destry came *here* – to Newell Farm?'

'Yesterday. Yes. He did.' The cows all nodded in their different ways. Someone who didn't know them might have thought that they had an itch, but Jamie knew they were nodding. 'He talked to

Farmer Willis,' murmured the cows. 'We liked what he said about spacing in dairy parlours. Plus we like the taste of his jacket.'

'Excuse me?' Jamie boggled. 'You're supporting Wilfred Destry because you like the *taste of his jacket*?'

There was more to it than that, Jamie knew. The cows had thought long and hard. It had been a long struggle, particularly when he'd read them the Green Party Election Pledge and had left them to think it over, but at last he had a result. The cows had come out for Wilf Destry. Wilf Destry was all right – official. His Review of Battery Farms proved it. He bothered to visit and see for himself, he was a man who liked and understood animals, anyone could see, plus the taste of his tweedy jacket was in there somewhere. He wasn't the world's greatest driver, but no one was perfect, the cows understood, not even Rameses the bull, perfect in every other way, but totally hopeless with gates.

'They've thought about the issues and they support Wilf Destry,' Jamie told his dad firmly.

'Destry's all mouth and trousers – that's what your mother says, anyway.'

'But what do *you* think – really?'

'I think Destry's all right. He's bothered to come round and meet everyone, which is more than the others've done. He knows what the problems are, locally. He'll do his best to fix them.'

'That's what *they* think – the cows, I mean.'

'Jamie, a joke's a joke.'

'And they've offered to wear, you know, posters and stuff.'

'Posters?'

'Yes, you know – "DESTRY RIDES AGAIN."'

'*Posters on cows?*' Jamie's father frowned. 'I think you'd better lie down.'

'That's what they do a lot,' Jamie said. 'But they still think the same way after. Give them a chance,' Jamie said. 'They want to get involved.'

'Cows? Wearing *posters?*'

'Why not?' Jamie wanted to know. 'They stand in fields, don't they? Everybody *sees* them. It's no different from postering a window or the back of someone's car. They want to help. I've got the posters,' Jamie went on, 'they asked me to get some last week. All I need is permission and *major* wallpaper paste.'

'Baler cord, more like,' his father said. 'You could tie on posters with baler cord, if they'd let you, I suppose. You'd have to ask Mr Willis. Those cows belong to Newell Farm.'

'I know that,' Jamie said. 'They told me that last week.'

'What else did they tell you last week?' His father looked at Jamie.

Jamie met his father's eye. 'I don't know. I've forgotten.'

'Tell me, are goldfish voting?'

'I wouldn't know.' Jamie read the warning signs. 'I never talk to goldfish.'

Two days later Jamie Sleep met Farmer Willis in the lane – either going to, or coming from, the cows. Jamie'd never seen him *there*, although he must've gone. The tractor slowed to let Jamie pass, and as it slowed Jamie saw something in its muck-splattered window which gave him the courage to stop it. The bright orange DESTRY sticker winking in the tractor-cab window filled him with strength of purpose. Wondering at what he was doing, instead of squeezing into the hedge, he waved Mr Willis down. 'Mr Willis,' he said, 'you know Wilfred Destry?'

'Destry! He's your man!' roared Willis, over his engine.

'Well, you know your cows down the road.'

'Heifers, is it?' Willis bellowed. 'I've just been down to see to 'em.'

'Well, did you think of posters?'

'Eh?'

'I SAID DID YOU THINK OF POSTERS,' Jamie screamed. 'POSTERS ON YOUR COWS, YOU KNOW – LIKE "DESTRY RIDES AGAIN"?'

For a moment Jamie Sleep wondered what he'd done. Farmer Willis changed colour from red to purple. He idled his engine and turned away. Finally, he gurgled. 'Naw,' he said at last. 'I never did think o' that. Jamie Sleep, isn't it?'

'That's right.'

'Posters on cows is a new one on me. Did you think o' anything else?'

Jamie took his courage in both hands. 'They want mucking out more often,' he said.

'How's that?' Willis cupped his ear.

'The cows,' Jamie said, 'down the road. Want mucking out more often.'

Willis's jaw dropped. 'Well, then, *you* got a lot to say for yourself.'

'People think they're stupid, you see. But they aren't really stupid at all. So do you think you will?'

'Will?'

'Muck them out more often.'

Willis revved his engine. 'I should think they might eat 'em, shun't you?'

'Eat?' Jamie shrank back in the hedge. 'Sorry, eat what?' he shouted.

'POSTERS!' Farmer Willis roared. 'POSTERS ON COWS – THEY'D EAT 'EM!'

Probably they would, Jamie thought. Farmer Willis was right. If you tried to tie posters on cows probably they'd pull 'em off, then they'd swallow the baler cord and get some frightful intestinal illness that involved lancing their stomachs with a knife. He watched the tractor roar off up the lane, with a catch in his throat all the same. He'd spoken up. He'd done his best. So why didn't he feel any better?

Hadn't he done what he could for the cows he represented, in the real world of getting-along-with-other-people and not-sticking-your-nose-in and never-speaking-out-of-turn and all the rest of it? Politics. Jamie sighed. He didn't envy Wilf Destry. It wasn't an easy job.

Jamie Sleep rested his head on the top of the concrete-block wall.

'Have you voted yet?' he joked, but the cows had eating in mind. 'Never mind,' he said. 'I voted for you. I made Mum vote for Wilf Destry — it's what you wanted, isn't it?'

The cows munched on, not listening.

'She said he was all mouth and trousers, but I said, you can't be serious. You can't vote for anyone else. Not Gerard Hopkins, no *way*.'

The DESTRY RIDES AGAIN posters fluttered over the cowsheds and snapped and bellied in the wind. Inside the cowsheds, a thick layer of fresh straw over a newly disinfected concrete floor made a clean and comfortable bed for some of the cleverest cows in the whole of the county.

'So in the end, she voted Wilfred Destry. Want to know what happens when you vote?'

Willis had been as good as his word. He'd told Jamie's father to tell him — Jamie — he was postering the shippen. *That boy*, he said, *he got it made. That boy's a laugh a minute.* As well as postering the cowsheds, Mr Willis had cleaned them out. *That boy's priceless*, he said. *Posters on cows. I never laughed so much since Derrick come out with no trousers.*

'What happens is, you go in and say your name in the village hall? Then Miss Rundle coughs all over you and finds it in the register and crosses out your name, see, so you can't vote twice?'

The cows munched their cow-cake contentedly. Jamie knew they were listening.

'Then what you do is you go in this, like, *booth* – like a wardrobe, only it's open? And inside it there's a shelf with a piece of paper and a pencil tied to a string and nothing else. And it smells of Chapel – the booth, I mean – 'cos that's where they brought it down from. And you turn the paper over, so then it's got their names on – Hopkins, Winfrith, Reardon, Destry – and you get the pencil on the string and you do a cross – it has to be a cross *not anything else at all*, or it doesn't count – and you do a cross in the box next to DESTRY, and then you fold it ONCE and drop it straight in this black tin box like a post-box. And Miss Rundle, she sniffs a bit, 'cos she can't hardly tell what you voted, and she doesn't like it very much. And then you say, "That's *that* done," and Mr Jago laughs. And then you go out an' you've voted.'

Wisdom the cow belched gently. Her blue-brown eyes regarded Jamie wistfully. But Jamie knitted his brows.

'Hope he wins the seat, don't you? It's a lot of trouble for a *seat*,' Jamie said. 'I should think it'd be easier to buy one.'

SEVENTH HEAVEN

You know those adverts where someone bites into a chocolate bar and then they're in heaven, or something? Or they buy a new car and drive off into the sunset with sappy smiles on their faces? Or their life is complete with a soft drink, or they're in paradise with a Bounty?

My idea of heaven is Alton Towers on a stomach stiff with pizza. Or paint-gunning in ninety-quid trainers and not caring if they get hit because I can buy some more. Or *three strikes* in a row. Or duffing in Kenneth Sweeney. Conclusively. Or blowing a thousand pounds in PC World. Or having a blast on those jet-skis. Or Christmas every day, which would be *cool*.

Seven heavens, it's not much to ask. Supposing one day it all happened, and not in an advert? I mean, *supposing adverts came true*? Would that be wild, or what? They came true for me, no kidding. You don't believe it happened? Imagine all the things you want. Then imagine having them — whatever you want, six times over, then one more time after *that*. Why d'you think they *call* it seventh heaven?

It started with my sister. My sister Eve's mad. She spends her dosh on clothes and expensive make-up. I wouldn't mind but she spends hours doing it, and you can't tell she's got it on. It's all like, down-to-earth eye-colour or hint-of-invisible face-gunk, or simply natural nails. Simple's the word. It costs her a mint, and you can't even see what it *is*.

But my sister listens to adverts. She pretends she doesn't, but she does. I don't, but she says I do. We had this argument about it. The argument went like this:

'I don't.' (Me.)

'You *do*.' (Her.)

'*You* do, you mean.' (Me, scoring points.)

'Oh, and you don't?' (Her, quite vicious.) 'Puh-lease. *You're just as bad as I am.*'

'Yeah, right, I don't *think* so.' (Me, arms folded, ironic.) '*I* don't buy scent called Excess at ten quid a bottle.'

'It's called perfume, thank*s* very much.'

'Should be called Waste of Space or Blow All Your Money.'

'Oh, and you're so choosy? You don't get things you see?'

'No, I get what I need.'

'You don't.'

'I do.'

'You get what everyone *else* gets.'

'I get what's cool, OK? I don't buy rubbish, all right, just 'cos it's hyped on the telly or in some girls' magazine.'

'Picky, picky, Mr I-get-whatever-hideous-stuff-my-*mates*-get. Like, you'd *know* what's cool, Mr I-don't-waste-my-money.'

She's right, I don't waste my money. The thing is, I'm quite tight. That's what really gets her. I dress casual, not flash, and I always have money for bowling, Burger King, whatever, while she blows all of hers. She's permanently skint is Eve, even though she works Saturdays, because whatever she earns she spends right away on the latest invisible make-up or some see-through shirt the weight of a leaf she's seen in some magazine.

So later I'm doing some homework, just enough to annoy me that I can't get through it really quickly before Man U play the cup this evening, when Evie bursts into my room with a pile of ripped-out adverts from magazines she found somewhere.

She throws them down. Is she *angry*. 'All right,' she says, 'let's see you look through *those* and say you're not.'

'Earth to Eve – not what?'

'Influenced by adverts. Let's have a look in here.' She rips open my clothes cupboard and starts shouting out brand-names in case she might *actually* be losing an argument: 'Optimum. Gearz. Stretch-7. The Heat. Banco-Banco. Hi-Tek. What a surprise. All makes you see in *ads*, plus how you think *these* –' (my trainers) 'how you think *these* are so great just 'cos David *Coutts* had some –'

Enough's enough. I get up and show her the door. 'Can you get out? The match is on in a minute.'

'So much for Mr Cool.' Hot under the collar, she's boiling. 'With his Laser Spot Stick next to his bed and his Free the Spirit deodorant. He doesn't watch adverts, oh, no.'

'You made your point. Bog off.'

Eventually she does. But not before she's slammed my cupboard door and thrown magazines all over my room. I flip on my telly and set up my snacks for the game. Then I have this stupid accident while I'm trying to adjust the aerial. Basically, I'm backed up behind my bedroom door with the aerial in my hand, waving it around, trying to get a picture that lets me see soccer instead of snow, when suddenly bam! This box of crap on my cupboard falls off and hits me WHUMP on the head and I'm seeing stars.

For a second I blank out totally. Then I'm, like, on the floor with all this stuff all over me. Stuff like old football boots, my Year 7 woodwork project, books, roller-blades, a few games that weigh, like, a ton, and anything *else* heavy you can think of. A pretty big box of stuff, the kind you wouldn't really want on your head. No wonder it hurt. I could always fill it with hammers for an encore. I stagger across to the mirror and look at my head. I'll live, but I'm not any prettier. It hurts like hell, if you want to know. Really good, Eve, I'm thinking. Thanks for shaking my cupboard up, so stuff falls off it and hits me. Thanks a million. Any time. I'd do the same for you.

So I'm sitting on my bed and I'm finally ready for the game. Fifteen minutes to go. A reasonable picture, at last. Pringles. Chocolate fingers. Marshmallows. Kola. Sorted. I have this massive headache, but so what? The ad-break before the game comes up, and the ads look really smart. Maybe I'm a bit light-headed, but for some reason I think I'll list them:

Lobo – the Classic Mint.

In the Mix '97 – thirty-three monster club hits.

Cap-n O'Reilly's Vegetable Sausages – you won't know you're not eating meat.

Mouth Hygiene from Dentiflex – more than just a toothpaste.

MAD RHINO! – When nothing can stop the charge! At cinemas near you!

Diet Kola – I don't want you . . . to be no slave . . .

Rodeo Jeans – as worn by people with shattered bones and not a lot of sense.

I switch channels for more ads, I'm not sure why. I start to notice the magazine ads my sister threw over the floor. They're for a range of products . . .

UFO chocolate Big Bar, Deep Star multimedia, Ray-Bans, Pentium Max, Optimum Active-wear, Aqua-dash surf-rider, Coolpak Venture, Nebula watches, Kawasaki Watercooled

Engineering, Virtual Fighter Systems USA, Zero-Shock Flare! – the Watch that Lights Up when you Press It.

...a range of products my sister knows I *like*. Nice one, Eves. She's only gone out of her way to get the kind of ads she thinks *influence* me, as if. I thought they'd be out of her magazines. But there isn't a natural whatsit or a down-to-earth thingummy among 'em. It's all cool stuff, you know. Stuff I wouldn't mind *having*.

I lay out the photo-spreads in a row. There are some duds, admittedly. Some cars I can live without. Some things I don't like at all. But, I have to admit, she makes a convincing point. Almost all the stuff I see, I want, and most of the stuff I want I can see in these glossy spreads . . . luring me into ad-land . . . enjoy, they say, enjoy . . . enjoy all the stuff you can see . . .

So my head's pounding and I'm crawling around on the floor looking at all these *pictures* of, like, torn silk and cactuses and cars with robots in them –

– and I'm arranging them into this, like, story –

– because some of them *are* pretty cool –

when

suddenly

I'm in this bar in cool Rodeo Jeans and this guy walks up, he looks like the guy in the Kola ad, and he wipes the sweat off his face and he sets down these crates and all the girls love him, you can see. And he buys me this drink that takes us off to some psychedelic beach with drums and hula skirts and cascades of ice in long tall glasses filled with lemons, and he says to me, 'Want to drive this car? You're in seventh heaven.'

And I go, 'What car?'

'This car.'

And I go, *'Whaa-aat?'*

'It's yours,' he says, 'we're in ad-land.' And he hands me these keys. 'Anything you want, times seven.'

And suddenly I'm driving this bright red Testarossa through white-walled canyons at about a hundred and twenty miles an hour, and at first it's too much, and I say: *'Too much!'* And old Kola Ad, he just smiles. But after a while it *is* too much, and after I do the hairpin the seventh time I can't hold it any longer, and I'm about to take a dive or whatever, when he shows me the bike.

The Kawasaki 1100 gleams in the sunshine like a dream. I'm riding it in an instant, and feeling the breeze, you know, as we top out at ninety on the bends. Again I'm feeling like paradise is just around the corner, except that the *same corner* comes at me *seven times*, again and again and again and again and again and again, so then I slam on the brakes and say, 'STOP!'

'Stop?' Kola guy raises an eyebrow.

'That's right,' I say. I stop the bike. 'You said, anything I want.'

'That's what I said.' And Kola guy gives me the nod.

'If that's what you *mean* –'

And I start to think. What ads do I like? What ads would I *die* to live in?

So I'm closing my teeth around this GIANT double cheeseburger, when the girl with the chewing gum gives me the secret smile, and next thing, I'm on the bus and we're sharing a stick between us, which is fine, until we drive into this town where everything looks off-kilter and kind of *wrong*. And we go into this supermarket where we soon get a chill to our bones when we realise we're in a sad grey town of sad grey people, living without the *only soft drink* that, you know, lights up the *world*.

Kola guy tips me the wink, and it's time to go.

Just then a puppy runs by covered in bog-roll, so I leg it down to the white cliffs of Dover to find it and catch a boxing match while I'm there, some flabby white guy in electric purple shorts shouting, *'Come on, we'll take you, what are you waiting for? You know when you've been Bongo'd!'* I turn round, and the girl off the bus is still there, but this time she's eating this chocolate bar. She's cutting the spikes off a cactus. She's waving her scissors around.

Then I'm six miles high in a bright red armchair, falling, falling towards the earth far below and the wind, it's battering my face so I can't even breathe, and the chair's *red* against the *blue* sky and it's plummeting down so fast the whole thing's in freeze-frame, and then we land PLUMP in some living room and FLUMP the cat lands on my lap. So I'm just stretching out to enjoy some TV dinners – whatever I want – when I see myself on the telly, OK, and I'm closing my teeth around this GIANT double cheeseburger, when the girl with the chewing gum gives me the secret smile and next thing, we're on the bus and we're sharing a stick between us, which is fine, until we drive into this town where everything looks off-kilter and kind of *wrong*.

And we go into this supermarket where we

soon get a chill to our bones when we realise we're in a sad grey town of sad grey people living without the only soft drink that, you know, lights up the *world*. Just then a puppy runs by covered in bog-roll, so I leg it down to the white cliffs of Dover to find it and catch a boxing match while I'm there, some flabby white guy in electric purple shorts shouting, '*Come on, we'll take you, what are you waiting for? You know when you've been Bongo'd!*'

I turn round, and the girl off the bus is still there, but this time she's eating this chocolate bar. She's cutting the spikes off a cactus. She's waving her scissors around. Then I'm six miles high in a bright red arm-chair, falling, falling towards the earth far below and the wind, it's battering my face so I can't even breathe, and the chair's *red* against the *blue* sky and it's plummeting down so fast the whole thing's in freeze-frame, and then we land PLUMP in some living room and FLUMP the cat lands on my lap. So I'm just stretching out to enjoy some TV dinners — whatever I want — when I see myself on the telly, OK, and I'm closing my teeth around this GIANT double cheeseburger—

'STOP NOW! I DON'T WANT TO!'

Kola guy gives me eyebrow.

'NO!' I'm shouting, really loud, 'CAN I *NOT* DO IT SEVEN TIMES!'

'You have to.' Kola smiles. 'This is Seventh Heaven.'

'I *DON'T* HAVE TO! AND I'M *NOT*!'

'Andrew!'

'SO DON'T EVEN TRY TO –'

'Andrew! Stop shouting!'

'*MAKE ME!*'

'Andrew – WAKE UP, YOU NIT!'

Mum's shaking me. I'm waking up. I think I'm on the floor.

'You missed the match,' she's saying. 'They beat them three-nil in the end.'

'Whadda say?'

'What are you doing rolling around with *magazines* stuck all over you?'

'Evie brought 'em in, I –'

'And *shouting* I don't-know-what.'

'I – um. I dunno.'

'You might want to take that picture off your face.'

I'm sitting up. I'm looking down. Why *have* I got ads all over me?

'I said, you missed the match. They won three-nil. How about some cocoa?'

'As long as it isn't *seven cups*.' I'm groaning.

The telly's on. The ads are up. *Chocolate Break. Take time out.*

'*Seven* cups of cocoa?' Mum looks me up and down like I grew an extra arm. 'What are you talking about?'

'I don't know.' I peel a picture off my face. 'I dunno what happened.'

'You fell asleep — what did you think? You really are odd these days, Andrew.'

Mum goes out to do stuff. I try putting off the telly, but as soon as I stand up my head hurts like *poo*. I feel the top of it carefully. A lump the size of Sunday. No surprises there. I look in the mirror and freak. There's only magazine newsprint all down one side of my face, plus the odd wild image from a photo. Bizarre. I look like an advert of *myself*. But when Mum comes back with the cocoa I know I'm real, if concussed.

'Is that a cut on your head?' she says. 'How did you *get* that cut?'

'That stuff on top of the cupboard?' I show her the stuff I mean. 'It weighs like a ton and *half*, and it only fell off and hit me after Evie slammed the door.'

'What did you argue about?'

'I dunno,' I said. 'Adverts.'

So then while she's sponging my head and putting on TCP, I say: 'Mum, if you went to heaven, what would it be like?'

She gets out the plasters and says, 'Let me see. A lovely white beach with pink shells and no one around – except someone way off in the distance, and you don't know who they are until they get close.'

'Dad?'

'Why spoil a nice idea?' Mum slaps on a plaster.

'Mum?' I ask her.

'What?'

'What's your favourite advert?'

'The one where Mum puts her feet up and does nothing and the family rally round and do all the washing, cooking and shopping and spoil her rotten?'

'What ad is that?'

'The ad I just made up.'

'Do I buy things in adverts?'

'Everyone does, don't they?'

'But I'm not like Eve, am I?'

'What's Eve like?'

'In heaven with purple nail varnish. Buying shoes to die for.'

'You're not as extravagant, no.' Mum laughs. 'Maybe you should be, though.'

'I should be extravagant?'

'Well, you know what they say. A little of what you fancy does you good.'

'But not *seven times* what you fancy. I don't fancy going to heaven,' I say, and my head's, like, giving me stick. 'I think heaven *sucks*.'

'What brought this on? A bang on the head?'

'Heaven's boring. Maybe,' I say, 'it's better the way things *are*.'

So a bang on the head knocked me out and sent me to ad-land. What do you want me to say? I realise how shallow I am? Nothing worth having comes easy? Kids these days know the price of everything and the value of nothing? They don't even know they're *born*?

Sorry, but it won't change a thing. Tight, I might be. Odd, like Mum says, I probably am. But I'm not in Seventh Heaven, you know? I'm actually back in real-time, where everything happens *once* so you better not blow it, and the car of your dreams takes a lifetime to earn but it's worth it when you get it. But, hey, I'm influenced by adverts. Just like anyone else. Thanks to Evie, OK, I know when I've been Bongo'd.

And ever after that, I want to say
be warned
ads are dangerous –
heavy stuff –
It's not all float away with an aero
in Seventh Heaven
– know what I mean?

But there's one thing I still don't get.
If Seventh Heaven can stress you out –
what about Cloud Nine?